His fingers itched to brush aside the strands of jet-black hair that clung in silky tendrils to her forehead and cheeks.

Six years had not marred the patrician perfection that was Patricia Hunter, thought Agent David Cassidy.

She had those same high cheekbones, delicate jaw and full lips. And he knew that beneath those thickly tipped lashes lay the most incredibly blue eyes he'd ever looked into. Eyes that could mesmerize a man's soul as easily as they haunted his mind.

But this no longer was the woman he had worshiped. The woman who had lain in his arms as they planned their future together—pledged their love to one another with words and their bodies. This was not the woman whose memory he'd fought unsuccessfully to exorcise from his heart.

The Trish Hunter he'd known no longer existed. The woman before him, Patricia Manning, was a stranger to him....

Dear Reader,

Let April shower you with the most thrilling romances around—from Silhouette Intimate Moments, of course. We love Karen Templeton's engaging characters and page-turning prose. In her latest story, *Swept Away* (#1357), from her miniseries THE MEN OF MAYES COUNTY, a big-city heroine goes on a road trip and gets stranded in tiny Haven, Oklahoma…with a very handsome cowboy and his six kids. Can this rollicking group become a family? *New York Times* bestselling author Ana Leigh returns with another BISHOP'S HEROES romance, *Reconcilable Differences* (#1358), in which two lovers reunite as they play a deadly game to fight international terror.

You will love the action and heavy emotion of *Midnight Hero* (#1359) in Diana Duncan's new FOREVER IN A DAY miniseries. Here, a SWAT cop has to convince his sweetheart to marry him—while trying to survive a hostage situation! And get ready for Suzanne McMinn to take you by storm in *Cole Dempsey's Back in Town* (#1360), in which a rakish hero must clear his name and face the woman he's never forgotten.

Catch feverish passion and high stakes in Nina Bruhns's *Blue Jeans and a Badge* (#1361). This tale features a female bounty hunter who arrests a very exasperating—very sexy— chief of police! Can these two get along long enough to catch a dangerous criminal? And please join me in welcoming new author Beth Cornelison to the line. In *To Love, Honor and Defend* (#1362), a tormented beauty enters a marriage of convenience with an old flame…and hopes that he'll keep her safe from a stalker. Will their relationship deepen into true love? Don't miss this touching and gripping romance!

So, sit back, prop up your feet and enjoy the ride with Silhouette Intimate Moments. And be sure to join us next month for another stellar lineup.

Happy reading!

Patience Smith
Associate Senior Editor

Please address questions and book requests to:
Silhouette Reader Service
U.S.: 3010 Walden Ave., P.O. Box 1325, Buffalo, NY 14269
Canadian: P.O. Box 609, Fort Erie, Ont. L2A 5X3

Reconcilable Differences

ANA LEIGH

Silhouette®

INTIMATE MOMENTS™

Published by Silhouette Books

America's Publisher of Contemporary Romance

SILHOUETTE BOOKS

ISBN 0-373-27428-9

RECONCILABLE DIFFERENCES

Copyright © 2005 by Anna Lee Baier

This edition published by arrangement with Harlequin Books S.A.

® and TM are trademarks of Harlequin Books S.A., used under license.
Trademarks indicated with ® are registered in the United States Patent
and Trademark Office, the Canadian Trade Marks Office and in other
countries.

Visit Silhouette Books at www.eHarlequin.com

Printed in U.S.A.

Books by Ana Leigh

Silhouette Intimate Moments

The Law and Lady Justice #1230
*Face of Deception #1300
*Reconcilable Differences #1358

*Bishop's Heroes

ANA LEIGH

is a Wisconsin native with three children and five grand-children. From the time of the publication of her first novel in 1981, Ana successfully juggled her time between her chosen career and her hobby of writing, until she officially retired in September 1994 to devote more time to her "hobby." In the past she has been a theater cashier (who married the boss), the head of an accounting department, a corporate officer and the only female on the board of directors of an engineering firm.

This *New York Times* bestselling author received a *Romantic Times* Career Achievement Award nomination for Storyteller of the Year in 1991, the BOOKRAK 1995-1996 Best Selling Author Award, the *Romantic Times* 1995-1996 Career Achievement Award and the *Romantic Times* 1996–1997 Career Achievement Award for Historical Storyteller of the Year. Her novels have been distributed worldwide, including Africa, China and Russia.

To Patti,
the heroine of all my novels.

Chapter 1

Patricia Manning leaned back in her chair and stared with contempt at the man seated opposite her. The audacity of Robert Manning held no limitations. "Go to North Africa with you! You are completely insane."

The mere sight of her husband turned her stomach, despite his suave handsomeness. Everything about Robert Manning was smooth, from the top of his three-hundred-dollar haircut to the tips of his imported Italian leather shoes.

"Now if you'll excuse me, I'm busy."

"You are so impetuous, my dear. At least listen to the proposition I have to offer before jumping to your usual hasty conclusions."

"Save your propositions for the hookers who service you, Robert."

His thin lips narrowed in an amused smile. "Still the

same uptight, frigid princess you always were, aren't you, Trish?"

"And you, Robert, are still the same perverted degenerate whom I can't bear to have touch me. Now that we've recounted both of our 'virtues,' let's not waste any more of my time. I have work to do. Good day."

He didn't budge when she reached for her telephone. "How badly do you want a divorce, Trish?"

What a joke that was! She paused dialing long enough to offer a contemptuous glance. "Some more of your sadism, Robert?"

"I'll give it to you if you go with me."

"Is this another of those cat-and-mouse games that you delight in playing, Robert?"

"I'm serious. It's important you go with me."

She replaced the phone in its cradle and leaned back in her chair. "Why is it so *important* I go with you?"

"Appearances. A lot's at stake here."

"Is this company business?"

"Certainly. Your father's aware of it. He thinks it's a good idea for you to go with me."

"He hasn't mentioned it to me."

"The situation just came up."

Trish picked up the phone and punched the quick dial to her father's personal line. After a quick conversation with him, she hung up and once again leaned back in her chair.

"When did you want to leave?"

"Friday."

"Separate rooms?"

"If you insist." His tone was as taunting as his smirk.

Trish still had reservations, but was so desperate to divorce him that the offer was tempting enough to make her consider. The last two years had been a nightmare.

She had found out on their honeymoon what a disastrous mistake she'd made marrying him. The six months that followed the wedding were the most degrading and embarrassing ones of her life. She had not let him near her since his perverted demands on their honeymoon and had immediately returned home and moved into a separate bedroom. To get even with her, he flaunted his mistresses in public, humiliating her at every opportunity.

Trish had wanted out of the marriage from the time they'd returned, but he had refused to give her a divorce and had threatened to expose her father's misdealings if she tried to divorce him.

To make the situation worse, her father had not denied the accusations when she confronted him with the threat; but he had told her nothing about his crimes other than that they would destroy his business and he'd end up in jail.

So she had continued to endure her marriage in name only because of her love for her father—the same reason she had forsaken her chance for happiness six years earlier. After six months, attempting to live under the same roof with Robert had become so unbearable she had moved back into her father's house.

This could be the opportunity she had hoped for—prayed for.

"All right, Robert, I'll agree, if you sign the divorce papers before we go."

"How do I know you'll keep your word if I do sign the papers?" he said.

Trish snorted. "Oh, please, Robert! We both know it's more likely I'll keep my word than that you would keep yours."

"Very well. I'll have Chandler draw them up."

"It won't be necessary to involve your lawyer. I had my attorney draw them up the day I moved out. All we have to do is sign and date them. We signed a prenuptial agreement before we married, we do not own any joint property, and even though you earn three or four times as much annually as I do, I am not asking for alimony. No strain or pain. Quick and painless."

"Painless?" He clutched dramatically at his chest. "How can you say that, dear wife, when you're breaking my heart?"

"Hardly, Robert. You don't have one."

She pushed a button on the intercom. "Libby, get my attorney, Carter Powell, on the phone."

Dave had a bad feeling about this mission. The expressions on the faces of the secretary general and deputy secretary only added to his unease; both Jeff Baker and Mike Bishop looked grimly contrite as they spelled out the mission.

"You saying you can't put us down any closer than five miles from the target?" Dave asked.

"I'm afraid not," Mike Bishop said. "We both agree a chopper could be seen and heard too easily if we got any closer. That would give the target a chance to get away. We figure the chopper can go in and lower you by rope, then pick you up again. And the closest position to try that is the coordinates we gave you."

Dave shook his head. "A five-mile hike with little cover. If there's a full moon, and luck is against us, we'll be spotted easily before we even reach bin Muzzar's palace. McDermott will be long gone by the time we do. That is *if* we do. Who in hell is this Colin McDermott anyway?"

"He belongs to a splinter group of the IRA. He murdered a member of the CIA in Belfast last month," Baker said. "Intelligence has traced McDermott to the home of Ali bin Muzzar in Northwest Africa. The Moroccan sheik's known to be sympathetic to the Irish cause, any terrorist cause for that matter. According to intelligence bin Muzzar has a private army of about two hundred. We're hoping you'll be able to get in and out without being observed or identified."

Yeah, right! Easy for you to say! Dave thought.

At that moment Baker's phone rang. After a short conversation the secretary general slammed the phone down and the ex-marine let out a string of expletives as long as his tattooed arm.

Dave and Mike Bishop exchanged meaningful glances. "Bad news, sir?" Bishop asked.

"Couldn't be worse. Intelligence just reported that in addition to McDermott, a Robert and Patricia Manning arrived today at the palace. Manning's an American businessman and a former Harvard classmate of bin Muzzar."

"You figure this Manning has a connection to the IRA?" Dave asked.

Baker shrugged. "Hard to say. His name or picture hasn't popped up on any database. Neither has his wife's. Could be just a matter of bad timing on this Manning's part. Try to avoid the couple."

Baker got up and walked around the edge of his desk to Dave. "Good luck to you and your squad, Agent Cassidy. We want this guy badly."

Dave recognized a dismissal when he heard one. He stood up, the two men shook hands, and then Dave headed for the door. Mike Bishop followed him out.

"So how's Ann?" Dave asked.

"Pregnant and contented—and even more beautiful.

I don't think Barney Hailey will ever get her back behind a camera again. She loves motherhood."

"And what about the impending father? How does he like the prospects of becoming a parent?"

"What do you mean prospects? I am a father. Brandon and I have a great relationship. I love the kid," he said, referring to the six-year-old Mike and Ann had legally adopted. "And I can't wait for our daughter to be born."

Dave shook his head. "Why can't I visualize you bouncing a baby on your knee?"

Chuckling, Mike slapped Dave on the shoulder. "Three more months, pal."

Then Bishop's grin faded. "Dave, be careful. Regardless of what Baker said, if it gets too hot, get out of there fast. We can get McDermott another time. What do you think of Addison?"

"Seems young."

"He's twenty-seven. That's older than some of us were when we joined."

"Right now I feel every day of my thirty-four years," Dave said. "The kid seems to get along well with the rest of the team. Since this is his first mission with us, I'll feel better when we get back."

Mike slapped him on the shoulder. "Hey, pal, didn't we all have to go through our first mission at one time or another?"

They shook hands and Dave headed back to where his squad waited to be briefed.

The following night as they neared the North African coastline Cassidy thought of that conversation with Mike Bishop. Addison looked nervous. But Mike was right. All the guys on the squad had gone through it. Besides, Bishop never would have assigned Addison to the squad if he didn't think the kid was ready.

Mike Bishop had been the leader of the Dwarf Squad, considered to be the elite special ops team of RATCOM—the Rescue and Anti-Terrorist unit of the CIA—until six months ago, when he'd been promoted to deputy secretary. At that time Dave had been moved up to squad leader.

The squad had been together for years. He, Bishop, Bolen and Fraser were all ex-SEALs. Williams and Bledsoe were Brits who had formerly served in England's SAS. They'd become a close-knit brotherhood and they trusted one another implicitly, in or out of combat.

Justin Addison had a rough road ahead of him before he'd gain that kind of trust from the squad. He'd grown up in the Bronx and was street-smart and tough enough physically, but it was yet to be proven if he had the kind of smarts needed for the job. It took a lot more than just physical strength and courage to be on a special ops squad. And even though he had trained with the navy SEALs for a year, he had never been on a mission, so he was still an unproven commodity as far as Dave was concerned. But Baker and Bishop must have seen something in Addison to offer him the opportunity to become a member of the CIA's legendary Dwarf Squad.

Well, Addison's first real test now lay ahead because there was no longer any time to ponder the issue. The airman opened the chopper door and dropped down two ropes. The squad moved to the door and lined up. Dave led off on one, Bolen on the other. Once on the ground they regrouped and within seconds were on their way.

* * *

When Trish came downstairs she was surprised to discover there were only four for dinner, and she was the lone woman. Had she known that, she would have feigned a headache and remained in her bedroom.

The other guest was an Irishman named McDermott. He was very reticent and made no attempt to join the dinner conversation. For that matter neither did she. Robert and Ali were doing all the talking.

As she observed them, she realized the three men were as different as day and night. She couldn't imagine what they might have in common.

Granted, Robert and Ali had been classmates at Harvard, but physically they were opposites. Robert was tall and blond, very handsome, suave and socially charming. It was these characteristics that had foolishly attracted her to him to begin with.

Ali, on the other hand, was dark, squat and obese, with a lecherous gleam in his dark eyes. She wanted to shower every time he looked at her. He made no attempt to conceal his attitude about women; one that she openly challenged. His amused smile always indicated how seriously he took her objections. The arrogant chauvinist was as obnoxious as Robert.

At least Colin McDermott appeared to find both Robert and Ali as unlikable as she did, as well as seeming anxious to get out of there. She couldn't fault him for that, since it paralleled her own thinking.

McDermott appeared to be about six feet tall with the pale skin of a redhead and a blue-eyed gaze that he kept shifting around. He looked like a trapped ferret. He expressed his impatience when Ali called for another bottle of wine.

"It'd be to my liking to be getting on with the business I've come here for," McDermott said. "I've given the diamonds to Manning to examine, and I'd like to finish the transaction and get out of here."

"I haven't had time to examine them, Mr. McDermott," Robert replied. "I'll do so first thing in the morning."

"Patience, my friend," bin Muzzar said to the Irishman. "Tomorrow we can conduct our business. Tonight we have the pleasure of a lovely dinner companion. We don't want to bore her with such mundane conversation."

"Then I'll be going to my room. I want an early start in the morning, bin Muzzar." The Irishman stomped off without any attempt at graciousness.

"I have to say, Ali, your friend is not much for manners," Robert said.

"But he makes sense," Trish said. "I would like us to have an early start tomorrow, too, Robert. So I think I will retire to my room."

"Oh, not until you taste this wine, my dear," bin Muzzar said. "It's been aged to perfection." He poured some wine into a silver goblet and handed it to her, and then filled his and Robert's goblets.

"To a very pleasant evening that can only become more delightful," he said.

"Here, here!" Robert said in agreement.

Trish's gaze swept the room over the top of the silver goblet as she took a sip of the vintage wine. Bin Muzzar's palace was a mixture of wealth and tastelessness.

Exquisite Oriental rugs embellished the fastidious marbled floors. Stained glass beautified most of the windows. In direct contrast, gold-encrusted nude figures of males and females in various stages of congress lined the sixteen-foot-high dome ceiling supported by ornamental pillars and columns adorned with leafy vines of woven gold.

Pure decadence! At best it resembled something out of a cheap Hollywood *Arabian Nights* production, or the garish interior of a Las Vegas hotel.

She shifted her glance to Robert. He'd already had too much to drink. So had the sheik. Old classmates! Birds of a feather! No wonder they got along so well.

Trish had met Ali only once before when he had come to the United States to be Robert's best man at their wedding. The night before the wedding the loathsome little toad had tried to hit on her, even though she was to become the bride of his dear classmate the next day. When she had complained to Robert about it, he'd merely laughed and shrugged it off. That should have been the warning sign to her. On their wedding night, Robert had suggested a ménage à trois with Ali. When she refused, he and his dear classmate left to spend the night with one of Robert's former girlfriends.

Trish thought of the painful days that followed. Of course Robert had claimed he had been too drunk to know what he was doing, and had begged her to forgive him. She had naively believed him.

Now, finally, after two miserable years of having to bear the embarrassment of being his wife legally, she'd have her divorce. Signed, sealed and hopefully filed— by the time she got back. She had honored her word and accompanied him here, but why it was so important to do so was still a mystery to her.

Trish took another sip of the wine. As soon as she finished it, she would go upstairs to her room. The two old classmates could stay up all night drinking and talking about old times as far as she was concerned.

"If you'll excuse me, gentlemen, I have a headache, so I'll retire for the night."

"I'm sorry to hear that, darling," Robert said. His concerned look was a convincing act, but it was wasted on her.

Trish stood up, and her knees buckled. Robert grabbed her arm before she could fall. "Let me help you, darling."

"I'm fine," she said, jerking free from him. His touch repulsed her.

"I insist."

Robert took her arm again. The room began to spin and she found herself unable to walk. Ali came over and took her other arm.

"Let me be of assistance, my dear."

Trish had never felt like this before. She had no strength in her arms and her legs could not support her. Unable to walk, she was forced to allow the two men to literally carry her.

"I'm so sorry," she murmured. "I don't understand. I feel as if I'm drug—"

The truth hit her and she felt the rise of panic. "No, let me go," she cried. "What are you doing to me?" She tried to struggle, but it was useless. By now she couldn't even raise an arm.

Robert laughed, and lifted her into his arms. "We wouldn't want to disappoint our gracious host, darling. He's been looking forward to this evening for the past day and a half. Haven't you, Ali?"

Bin Muzzar laughed. "More like two years, my friend. Normally, Patricia, I'm not this patient waiting for a mere woman, but Robert promised me the wait would be worthwhile. Despite your current condition, I am sure, my dear, you will enjoy what is to come as much as we will."

She tried to scream, but even her vocal chords were paralyzed. Her voice was barely louder than a murmur. "Let me go. You can't do this. Robert. Please."

"Since our marriage will be severed, darling, I can't think of a fonder memory to carry with me when we go our separate ways."

She managed a weak scream when they reached her room, but it was drowned out by the laughter of the two men as Robert carried her to the bed.

Trish felt herself slowly begin to slide into unconsciousness and prayed for the merciful darkness to overcome her swiftly. But for now she could only lie helplessly, staring up, horrified, into the lascivious faces of the two men who had begun to strip her of her clothing.

They pivoted in surprise when the door suddenly burst open. Through her drugged haze she imagined the face on the tall figure in the entrance—an image that had haunted her conscience, as much as her dreams, for the last six years. Was he real or was this just a wishful figment of her imagination again?

Dave! her heart shouted joyously.

Help me, Dave. Please help me, Trish cried out in a soundless murmur before blackness enveloped her.

Chapter 2

Dave stared at the two men. He recognized bin Muzzar from his picture at the briefing, but the other man was not McDermott. From his coloring and clothing, Dave figured the second man had to be the American, Robert Manning. He was aware of a woman on the bed but ignored her. None of these three people were his target.

Up to now, there was no way bin Muzzar would know he was an American. He wore dark clothes and his face was covered with greasepaint in the hope of not revealing his nationality, since the British government was after the terrorist as well as the CIA. The sheik would have no way of knowing for certain who was behind the raid. The less said, the better.

In Arabic, Dave asked bin Muzzar which room McDermott was in.

Bin Muzzar turned on Manning and issued a string

of curses accusing him of betrayal. Manning attempted to deny them, but bin Muzzar did not believe him and warned Manning he'd pay for his treachery. He then strode from the room and Cassidy followed.

The sheik was further incensed when he saw the rest of the squad. Their presence set him off into another tirade and, ranting violently about the armed invasion of his home, he led them to a closed door at the end of the hall.

Dave didn't like the situation at all. The mission was taking too long. It was too noisy. The whole damn palace had to hear bin Muzzar shouting at them. And they were on the second floor—a definite disadvantage if the sheik's army became involved and put up a resistance.

To shut bin Muzzar up, Dave made a threatening motion with his rifle, and the sheik drew back and quieted. However, by this time the damage had been done. There was no doubt in Dave's mind that McDermott couldn't have helped hearing the commotion, and would probably be waiting with a weapon in hand.

Dave turned the handle. The door was unlocked. He shoved it open and then ducked back. When there were no shots fired, he cautiously peered in. The room was dimly lit, but it appeared empty.

One by one the men slipped into the room. The bed showed signs of having been used, McDermott's backpack was still in the room, but there was no sign of the Irishman.

"Dammit!" Dave cursed when he discovered that bin Muzzar had slipped away, too. A quick check of the remaining rooms on the floor produced the same results. No McDermott or bin Muzzzar. They were all empty except for the one that Manning and the woman were in.

"What now?" Don Fraser asked.

"We get the hell out of here," Dave said.

"Shouldn't we search the rest of the palace for him?" Addison spoke up.

"How long you figure that would take, sonny?" Bledsoe asked.

"We've wasted enough time. Grab McDermott's pack and let's get out of here."

At that moment Manning came running down the hall. "You've got to help me. Ali thinks I've double-crossed him and that I'm working with you. I know him, he'll kill me."

"Suck it up, pal," Dave said. "In the future, I'd be more selective whom you pick for a friend."

Manning looked desperate. "I can tell you're an American. My name is Robert Manning. I'm an American citizen. I demand your help."

"We're not the Red Cross, Manning."

The whole mission had turned into a disaster. But, no matter how Manning was involved with bin Muzzar, Dave knew he couldn't leave an American citizen to the mercy of the sheik.

"What about your wife, Manning?"

"Ali won't hurt her," Manning said.

"Where is she now?"

"She's the woman in the bed."

"You mean the woman you two were about to…? Seems we spoiled your plans for the night." He couldn't stand to look at the bastard. "Hurry up and get her out here."

"There's a problem," Manning said. "She's had too much to drink. She's passed out."

"Then carry her. We're getting out of here now."

Manning rushed back to the room and while they waited, Dave pulled the squad together.

"The mission's fallen apart. Bin Muzzar's probably

alerted the palace guard by now. Most likely we'll have to fight our way out. Addison, you'll probably have to carry the woman. That SOB she's married to isn't worth a damn. Get Manning and his wife out of here now. If they're not ready, leave them behind. Bledsoe and Williams, take the point."

The two men moved ahead cautiously. The lower floor appeared deserted. Dave had no idea where the sheik had disappeared to. Undoubtedly he had gone for help.

"Bolen and Fraser, cover Addison," Dave ordered when the others came out of the bedroom. Addison had the woman slung over his shoulder. Dave had started down the stairway when Williams gave them an all-clear sign. He was followed by Addison who carried the woman. Manning was beside Addison. Bolen and Fraser brought up the rear.

They made it out of the building without encountering any servant or armed opposition and moved cautiously toward the gate in the stone wall surrounding the palace. There was no sign of the gatekeeper.

Dave halted them in the cover of some trees in the garden. "Stay alert," he ordered. "This reeks of an ambush."

"Why not engage us before we're out of the gate?" Bolen said.

"Most likely bin Muzzar doesn't want any damage done to his palace," Dave replied. "They're probably waiting to hit us when we're in the open."

"Maybe the sheik hasn't had time to organize his men yet?" Fraser said hopefully.

"We can only hope," Dave mumbled.

"Why have we stopped? Let's get out of here," Manning blurted out, interrupting them.

"Shut your mouth, Manning, and get back where

you belong," Dave declared. He'd loathed the bastard on sight. His presence at the palace at the same time as McDermott was no coincidence. Bin Muzzar's outburst had revealed Manning and he were involved in some kind of foul play. Financing terrorists, no doubt. On top of that, even though Dave was no moralist, the two of them playing sex games with the guy's wife disgusted him, even if the woman had apparently cooperated. So much for the mother of your child. Maybe they didn't have any children. A blessing if they didn't. People were becoming sicker by the day. It was no wonder the world was so damn fouled up.

He shrugged aside his wayward thoughts. Why in hell was he moralizing? The damn fool things that went through a man's head when he's scared were ridiculous. Their sex lives weren't his problem. Getting his squad out of this mess was.

"All right, let's move out. Bledsoe, Williams." The two men nodded and Dave watched them shift from tree to tree as they worked their way to the gate. Seconds passed like hours as he waited for a sudden outburst of gunfire. His grasp loosened on the rifle he clutched, and he wiped his sweating palm on his pants leg, then shifted the weapon to the other hand and did the same.

Williams reappeared at the entrance of the gate and waved them on. They moved out.

Once they cleared the gate, they broke into a run. The extra hundred-plus pounds Addison was carrying didn't appear to slow his stride. Now it was a foot race to cover the five miles and get back to the extraction point. There was no doubt in Dave's mind that bin Muzzar would pursue them. Fraser's guess was right, he was obviously rallying his army.

At least the terrain was flat and they were making

good time. They got another break when the moon disappeared behind drifting clouds. It was a temporary respite, but he welcomed any help he could get. They were nearing the coast when the moon's silver rays once again streaked the countryside just as they heard the distant sound of approaching vehicles. AK-47 cartridges had begun kicking up puffs of dirt around them by the time they'd reached the cover of the rocky coastline.

"What in hell should we do?" Bolen shouted as bullets ricocheted off the rocks around them.

"Take cover and hold your fire."

At that moment a rocket-propelled grenade exploded nearby.

"Now they're launching RPGs at us and we aren't supposed to shoot back?" Addison shouted.

"We've got no choice now," Dave said. "We'll have to take out the ones with the RPGs before they blow us apart. No spraying. Use your rifles' laser low lights and thermo-sightings to pick your targets."

A bullet ricocheted off a nearby rock. "How are we going to get out of here?" Addison shouted, trying to be heard above the steady clatter of gunfire. "They'll pick us off like fish in a barrel."

"Just hold them back until I can get us some help."

Dave pulled out the encrypted cell phone. Knowing that everything he said would be scrambled into code during the transmission, he identified himself and their coordinates, and then shared the bad news.

"We're in the rocks and taking heavy fire from RPGs and AK-47s to our west." Another grenade exploded nearby to reinforce the seriousness of his report. "We need close air support. We have two American civilians with us. Repeat. We need close air support."

"We're gonna be out of ammo before any help can

reach us," Addison mumbled a short time later as he changed the clip in his rifle. "This is my last clip."

"What are we going to do?" Robert Manning cried out. He appeared on the verge of hysteria.

Dave tossed Addison one of his remaining clips, and then glanced with loathing at Manning huddled behind the shelter of a boulder.

Addison had placed Manning's wife under the same shelter. She was lying unconscious on her stomach. Her cowardly husband wasn't making any effort to protect her body from a possible ricochet.

"Was she hit?" Dave asked.

"No, sir," Addison said. "She's been out cold since before we even left the palace. I ain't seen her move a muscle or heard a peep out of her."

"It shouldn't be much longer. When I contacted them, they'd already launched a couple of F/A-18s from a carrier in the Mediterranean."

Dave had no sooner uttered the words when two low-flying jets screamed past, the red glare of their backburners welcome fiery beacons overhead. Dave flashed the signal to identify their position and the jets circled and flew past again.

"What if they start firing at us?" Manning said. "You hear about friendly fire all the time."

If the bastard didn't shut up, it sure as hell wouldn't be friendly fire that killed him.

"Don't sweat it, Manning. They've got a GPS fix on us now."

"What's that?" Manning asked.

"A global positioning satellite," Kurt Bolen said quickly to shut Manning up. "Those pilots know exactly where we are now."

Infrared sights exposed the position of the attackers

and the pilots opened up with their guns, spraying the ground ahead of them with a warning hail of bullets.

It was enough to rout the pursuers. Before the jets could circle again, the roar of the retreating car engines signaled the battle's end.

Dave had just gotten the all-clear sign on the phone when the sudden whir of rotors announced the arrival of a helicopter.

Within minutes they were airborne, and Dave contacted Mike Bishop.

"The mission was a bust, Mike. The target escaped."

"Did you all make it out okay?"

"Yeah. No casualties."

"Why in hell did you kill bin Muzzar?" Mike asked. "He wasn't your target."

"He's dead? It wasn't intentional. We were taking heavy fire from RPGs and AK-47s. All we were doing was holding them off."

"According to our sources the sheik died at the palace. His throat had been cut."

"Then it wasn't one of us."

"Maybe McDermott killed him. Figured it was a double cross."

"Could be. Bin Muzzar accused Manning of one before the sheik disappeared. That's why we had to bring out Manning and his wife. We did bring McDermott's pack with us. Maybe it will turn up something."

"Glad you're all safe. See you when you get back."

"Right. Roger and out."

Dave hung up the phone and shifted back to join the others. A couple of the men had already fallen asleep. Manning was sitting with his back against the wall chewing on his lip. He'd have a lot to explain when they got back to the States. He'd been consorting with a known terrorist. He was certain to pull some jail time for that. Dave hoped the government would lock Manning away and lose the key.

He wiped the greasepaint off his face and shifted over to Addison's side. The kid had done good. Followed orders and kept his cool under fire. But he looked so damn young. Right now Dave felt as old as Methuselah—or at least ancient enough to join the Rolling Stones.

"How's the lady doing?"

"She's been sleeping peacefully, sir."

"Through the whole thing?"

"Yes, sir."

"Well, Manning said she'd been drinking heavily and passed out."

"That's what he said, sir. But it sure doesn't seem right to me. She never moved a muscle even on the run." Addison glanced down at the woman. "She's the hottest woman I've seen in a long time. I'd have thought she could do better than that jerk she's married to."

"Birds of a feather, kid. You saw what we walked in on. Let this be a good lesson. Looks can fool you."

"Sir, please don't call me 'kid.'"

"It's a deal providing you quit calling me 'sir.'"

Addison grinned. "Clear, sir…ah, Dave."

"Now why don't you grab some shuteye? It's been a long day."

"Guess I will." Addison looked down again at the sleeping woman. "But she sure is hot, sir. 'Bout the prettiest I've ever seen." He shifted over, leaned back against the wall and closed his eyes.

Other than a quick glance in her direction when he'd entered the bedroom, Dave had not had a close look at Patricia Manning.

Curious, he leaned over to see if Addison had exaggerated. He sucked in his breath from the sudden punch to his gut when he recognized the face that had haunted him for the past six years.

Bombarded by memories, Dave stared transfixed at the woman. How often had he gazed down at that sleeping face? Caressed the softness of it. Breathed the intoxicating essence of her or tasted the sweetness of her lips?

Gradually, reasoning pierced the barrier of shock. He glanced around guiltily, thankful that no one appeared to be watching him. He knew he should move away, but he couldn't resist the tempting draw.

His gaze clung to her face. She looked ethereal in the dim light of the cabin. His fingers itched to brush aside several strands of jet-black hair that clung in silky tendrils to her forehead and cheeks.

Six years had not marred the patrician perfection of those same high cheekbones, delicate jaw and full lips. And he knew that beneath those thickly tipped lashes lay the most incredible blue eyes he'd ever looked into. Eyes that could mesmerize a man's soul as much as they haunted his mind, pierced his heart.

But this no longer was the woman he had worshipped from the moment they met. The woman who had lain in his arms as they planned their future together—pledged their love to one another with their words and bodies. The woman whose memory he'd fought unsuccessfully to exorcise from his mind and heart.

Trish Hunter no longer existed.

Now only this pathetic facade of that woman remained.

This woman was the wife of a loathsome cad. This woman consorted with terrorists. Indulged in sex orgies. Drank herself into oblivion.

This Patricia Manning was a stranger to him.

* * *

A faint roar slowly penetrated the dark void that swaddled her. The sound heightened as blackness slowly faded into a grayish haze and Trish struggled through it to regain consciousness.

With this slow return of her sensibilities came a feeling of uneasiness. Fright. Why? She strove to remember. Then the horror of it swept through her as leering images of Robert and Ali bin Muzzar swirled around in the muddled confusion of her thoughts like demonic specters.

The need to scream rose within her and a responsive spasm racked her spine. Overwhelmed with panic she opened her eyes. The scream froze in her throat, but this time it wasn't drugs that prevented the outburst; it was stunned recognition. She stared into the eyes fixed on her. Those beautiful, compelling brown eyes she remembered so well, had imagined before she passed out.

"Dave," she murmured softly.

There was shocked recognition in his eyes as he stared back at her. Was he all part of the same hideous nightmare?

"Manning, your wife's awake," he said, and moved away.

She'd know that voice anywhere—and that same hard tone he'd used the last time they'd spoken six years ago.

Trish closed her eyes and felt the salty sting of hot tears on her cheeks.

When Trish next awoke, the effects of the drug had worn off fully, and she became aware that she was in a helicopter about to land. For several minutes she remained lying still, trying to distinguish in her mind what had been real and what had been part of the nightmare.

She jerked up to a sitting position and looked around when she recognized Dave's voice. But what was happening? What was he doing issuing orders to a huddled group of men preparing to disembark. Could she still be dreaming?

She closed her eyes and pinched herself hard. It hurt and she opened her eyes. He was still here. She hadn't imagined it. It was true. Dave *was* here. Close enough to touch.

Shifting to her knees, she felt a thousand needle-pricks in her arms and legs. Now there was no doubt. She wasn't still dreaming, that was for sure. The pain was too intense to be imagined. She started to get up to shake it off.

"Ma'am, it's best you remain seated until we touch down," the man who sat beside her said.

"Where are we?"

"Rheinmein Air Base, ma'am, in Frankfurt, Germany."

"Germany!"

Their voices attracted Dave's attention and he glanced over to them. "Trouble, Addison?"

"No, sir. Mrs. Manning is awake and wanted to know what was happening."

Outside the plane, crewman swung the door open, and several of the men jumped out. The revolving red light of an emergency vehicle flashed through the opening and someone outside handed a stretcher into the helicopter.

"If you lie down, ma'am, we'll get you out of here."

"I don't need a stretcher," Trish said. "I'm fine, now."

She moved to the door, and as she tried to step down,

her knees buckled. She fell forward into Dave's out-stretched arms.

For a hushed moment they stared into each other's eyes, and she fought the urge to fling her arms around his neck and never let go.

"Mrs. Manning, there would be less chance of your getting injured if you would lie down on the stretcher," he said.

"I'll be fine. I just have to shake off the numbness."

Dave released her, and joined the squad who were piling into a military vehicle. Addison led her to a sedan, assisted her in and then joined his squad. Robert and two other men climbed in after her.

The car pulled out and the military vehicle followed behind. They drove to a building located right on the base.

Once inside, Trish was taken to an office where two men and a woman were waiting.

"How do you do, Mrs. Manning," one of the men said. "Please sit down." He nodded to the woman and she turned on a machine.

The woman identified herself, announced the date, time and location, and then said, "The following is an interrogation of Patricia Diane Manning. Present are Agent Roger Reteva, Agent William Moore, and Mrs. Patricia Manning."

To Trish's further surprise, the woman followed it with her father's Georgetown address. Why would these people know her father's address?

"Mrs. Manning, I'm Agent Reteva," one of the men said. "And this is my associate William Moore. We'd like to ask you a few questions if you don't mind."

"Who do you represent, Mr. Reteva?" Trish asked.

"I don't think that's germane to the issue, Mrs. Manning."

"I'm afraid I do. If you expect me to answer any of your questions you will have to answer mine first."

The two men at the table exchanged meaningful glances. "We're with the Central Intelligence Agency of the United States, madam."

Trish gasped in surprise. "The CIA? What is this all about?"

Reteva's lips curled in a slight smile. "That's what we are trying to find out, Mrs. Manning. Your name is Patricia Diane Manning?"

"Yes."

"Your maiden name was Patricia Hunter, and you're a citizen of the United States?"

"Yes, I am," Trish replied. "Will you kindly tell me why I'm being interrogated?"

"It is our understanding you were a house guest for the past two days at the home of Sheik Ali bin Muzzar. Is that correct, Mrs. Manning?"

"Yes."

"Was this a business or personal visit, Mrs. Manning?"

"I was told it was a business trip," Trish said. "Although, the sheik and my husband were classmates at Harvard University. It has been my impression that they have maintained a friendship since then."

"Were there any other guests present at the time?"

"Yes, a Mr. Colin McDermott."

"Had you met Mr. McDermott previously to that time?"

"No," Trish said.

"Was Mr. McDermott also a Harvard classmate of your husband?"

"I have no idea."

"A business associate?"

"I've never heard the name before, but it doesn't

rule it out since I'm not active in my husband's business affairs."

"Your husband is a vice president at the firm of Hunter International Banking Incorporated in Washington, D.C., is that correct?"

"Yes it is," Trish replied.

"And your father Henry Jonathan Hunter is the president and majority stockholder of that firm. Is that also correct, Mrs. Manning?"

"The last I heard he was," Trish said lightly, to disguise her irritation. She was thoroughly confused. Why was she being interrogated like a common criminal?

"It is our understanding that as American citizens, your life and that of your husband would have been threatened if you had remained at the home of Sheik bin Muzzar. Is that correct?"

"I don't know. I passed out. When I awoke, I was in a helicopter and on my way here."

"Before you 'passed out,' Mrs. Manning, did you witness any business exchange, conversation or threats between your husband, Ali bin Muzzar or Colin McDermott."

"No. On the contrary, my husband and bin Muzzar were close friends. I only met Mr. McDermott for the first time at dinner that evening. He retired to his room early because he said he intended to leave the following morning. I did the same." She could not embarrass herself by telling these strangers what had actually transpired between her and those two degenerates after McDermott had departed.

"And that was the last you saw of Mr. McDermott?"

"Yes."

"Thank you, Mrs. Manning, you've been most cooperative."

The woman turned off the machine, and the two men stood up.

"Until Sheik bin Muzzar's death is cleared up—"

"Ali is dead?"

"Yes, Mrs. Manning. Until we have all the details, you will have to remain in our custody. We will be returning you to the United States tomorrow."

"I don't understand, Mr. Reteva, am I under arrest?"

"Mrs. Manning, there has been a crime committed, so for the time being consider yourself under our protection. If you have been straightforward with us, you have nothing to worry about. Enjoy your brief stay in Germany, madam. If there is anything you need or wish, we are at your disposal." .

Trish was taken to a reception room where several of the squad were playing cards. There was no sign of Robert, but Dave was stretched out on a bench in a far corner with his eyes closed. She wanted some answers and wanted them now. She strode over to him.

"Dave, I want to talk to you."

He opened his eyes, gave her a disgruntled look and then sat up.

"What do you want?"

"What happened at bin Muzzar's palace after I passed out?"

"Hmm…let me think. Oh, yeah, your husband and his friend invited us to join the party, so the whole squad jumped you."

His sardonic smirk made her angrier than his words. "Your attempt at humor fails miserably, General Cassidy. I once believed that kind of humor was beneath you."

"I might say the same about you, Mrs. Manning. So it would seem we were both wrong about each other.

By the way, it's Agent Cassidy. I'm not in the military, Mrs. Manning."

He lay back down and closed his eyes.

"Agent? You mean you're one of these CIA agents, too?"

With a resigned sigh, he opened his eyes and sat back up. "I work for the CIA if that's what you're asking, Mrs. Manning. I'm not with intelligence."

"I think I have a right to know what went on there, since the CIA apparently believes I'm involved in the murder of Ali bin Muzzar."

"I can assure you, Mrs. Manning, you weren't. Bin Muzzar was still alive after you passed out. I informed them of that during the debriefing. Now, if you don't mind." He stretched out on the bench again and closed his eyes.

"I suppose your squad killed him?"

He stiffened with annoyance and sat up. "No, my squad did not kill him. Ask your husband, Mrs. Manning, maybe he can tell you."

"Are you saying Robert killed Ali?"

"I didn't say that. I can only tell you that the last time I, or any member of my squad, saw bin Muzzar he was still alive."

At that moment Robert Manning came into the room and took a seat. Trish made no move toward him, but went over and sat down on an empty chair.

They waited another half hour until all the squad members were debriefed, and then they were driven to a hotel.

Chapter 3

Trish balked when they started to assign her and Robert to the same room. She insisted upon a separate one and won the argument.

Once alone, she flopped down in relief on the bed. Despite everything that had happened in the past twenty-four hours, the hardest thing to bear was the change in Dave.

Seeing him again had been the answer to her prayers. But he was so different from the man she remembered. Granted, he had good reason not to greet her with open arms, but remembering the love and tenderness they had once shared, it was hard to believe he held so much bitterness toward her.

She yearned to sit down and just talk to him again. After all, even if they were ex-lovers, they also had been good friends. They had always enjoyed each other's company. They had not only loved each other, they had liked each other as well.

But now, she could see the loathing in his eyes when he looked at her. And that hurt. That hurt badly. She was helpless to avoid reacting negatively to it, so they'd ended up snarling at one another.

As if that wasn't staggering enough, there was all this mystery surrounding Ali's death. Could it be that Robert had killed Ali?

Trish shook aside the thought. Ali was probably the only friend Robert had. And although she held no one in lower esteem than Robert, she couldn't see him in the role of a murderer. Liar, conniver, rapist, yes. But murderer, no.

A light knock sounded on the door and the chambermaid came in.

"Frau Manning, I am Helga, the chambermaid. The gentleman in the next room told me to bring you these items." She handed Trish a brown paper bag.

"Thank you. Helga, I'm so sorry," Trish said, embarrassed. "I don't have a purse with me. Perhaps I can put a tip on the bill."

"That is not necessary, Frau Manning. The gentleman has taken care of it. If you need anything else, just ring for me. Have a pleasant evening, madam."

Trish gratefully dumped the goody bag on the bed and out dropped a plethora of useful items: a comb, shampoo, toothbrush, toothpaste, a compact of pressed face powder, a tube of lipstick, a pair of panties and a bra. There was even a black and white jogging suit in her size.

Trish was so grateful she could have shouted with joy, and the thoughtful gesture was so unlike Robert. As difficult as it would be, she would have to swallow her pride and thank him.

She gathered up several of the items and headed for the shower.

* * *

After fifteen minutes of hot water and swirling steam, Trish felt like a new woman. She dried off, combed her hair and while it dried, she rinsed out her underclothes and hung them up to dry.

As she struggled with the decision of whether to go down to dinner or settle for room service, the telephone rang.

"Mrs. Manning, this is Justin Addison. We're going down to dinner soon and Dave wants to know if you're ready."

"I was just considering ordering room service," she said.

"One moment, ma'am."

She could hear him consulting with someone in the background, then he came on the line again.

"Ma'am, Dave says that's not a good idea. We've been ordered to keep an eye on you, so if you don't go down to dinner, a couple of us will have to remain up there with you."

"And you'd have to be one of them, isn't that right, Mr. Addison?"

"I'm afraid so, ma'am," he said.

Apparently the decision had been made for her. "Okay, I'll be ready in five minutes."

The new underwear and jogging suit were a perfect fit. Leave it to Robert to be able to appraise a woman's figure.

She pulled her hair back into a plain ponytail and tied it with a piece of white ribbon that had been wrapped around the jogging suit. After adding a light dusting of powder to her nose and cheeks, a dash of gloss to her lips, she was ready when the rap came on the door exactly five minutes later.

Dave, Justin Addison and the agent they called Kurt Bolen were in the hallway.

"Gosh, gentlemen, are you sure three of you big, macho males are enough to keep li'l ole me from escaping?"

"I guess we'll just have to risk it, Mrs. Manning," Dave said. "Your husband preferred to eat earlier so we were forced to split up the squad."

She was pleased to hear she wouldn't have to have dinner with Robert. Two consecutive nights facing him across a table would have been a tough row to hoe. Granted, she was grateful for the goody bag, but it fell far short of erasing the sordid memories of the past two years.

Deciding to try a restaurant elsewhere, the group strolled along casually, peeking into shop windows. They finally settled on a quaint rathskeller several blocks from the hotel.

Despite her hunger, Trish was unable to finish the tasty baked apple stuffed with pork that she had ordered. The men however had no problem consuming large plates of thick slices of sauerbraten served with plump dumplings and steins of dark beer.

When it came time for dessert, Kurt insisted they order one called *Zwetschgenkuchen*. The guys went along with his selection, and as they drank steaming hot cups of strong coffee, the waitress brought them the dessert.

Trish already had had enough to eat, but Kurt insisted she try a small piece.

"You'll love it, Mrs. Manning. When I was young, I remember my German grandmother used to make it all the time. I haven't had a piece since she died."

Trish relented. "Well, out of respect to your dearly departed grandmother, Kurt, I'll take a tiny piece."

"This isn't bad," Justin declared after taking a hardy bite. "What am I eating?"

"It appears to be a puff pastry and the filling tastes like plum," Trish said.

"Trouble with plums, Mrs. Manning, no matter how juicy and sweet they taste, they shrivel up into prunes," Dave said.

The comment was too deliberate to be casual. Then she recalled he'd talked of plums and prunes the last time they'd made love. She raised her head and looked at him. His gaze was fixed on her. So he too was remembering that—and the tragic ending to that day.

"Don't you agree, Mrs. Manning?" he said.

"I suppose they do, Agent Cassidy. But at least they're sweet while they last." Right back at you, David Cassidy!

Trish raised the fork to her mouth and slipped a piece of the pastry between her lips.

"Dave, do you mind if the kid and I kind of check out the town for a little while?" Kurt said. "We'll be pulling out of here first thing in the morning."

"What time is your watch?"

"Not until midnight."

"Then you better make sure your butt's in that hallway when the clock strikes twelve."

"Thanks, sir," Justin said, jumping to his feet. "Let's go, Kurt."

"Are you ready to leave, Mrs. Manning?" Dave asked, after paying the check.

Now that they were alone, Trish was so tempted to challenge his attitude. To try and have him get out whatever was on his mind. But she just couldn't get the right words out either. They were at an impasse.

"Yes, any time you are."

Once outside they saw the weather had taken a turn for the worse. Fog had moved in, and it was difficult to see more than a short distance ahead.

"Our being alone puts you at a disadvantage, doesn't it, Agent Cassidy?"

"Now why would you think that, Mrs. Manning?"

"Aren't you afraid I'll try to escape?"

"It's not going to keep me awake worrying about it, if that's what you're implying."

"What reason would I even have to try?"

"I have no idea. You brought it up, Mrs. Manning."

"And even if I'd succeed, what good would it do? I don't have anything except these clothes on my back."

She was babbling and she knew it, but she was too nervous to remain quiet.

"Glad to see they fit."

The truth hit her like a lightning bolt. She stopped abruptly. "So it was you!"

"What?"

"You're the one who got me this jogging suit and the other supplies."

"Somebody had to do it."

She should have guessed from the beginning that Robert would never consider anyone's interests but his own. "Thank you, Dave. It was very thoughtful of you."

"Don't blow it out of proportion, Mrs. Manning. I'd have done the same for anyone. You're under my protection."

"Protection? I'd say it's more like under suspicion, Agent Cassidy. Prisoner, more realistically. Where do you think I could go? I have no passport, money, charge card or identification. I don't even have the money to make a phone call."

"You could always call Daddy collect. I'm sure he'd

send the corporate jet to slip in under the radar and rescue his little princess."

"Do you really hate us that much, Dave?"

"I don't hate anybody, Mrs. Manning. Not you, your father or that schmuck you married. I'll just be glad when all of you are out of my life."

His cell phone suddenly beeped and he pulled it out of his pocket.

"Sneezy here," Kurt Bolen said, using the code name the agency had assigned him. "Looks like you've picked up a friend. We've got a make on a guy who appears to be following you."

"Give it to me."

"Five eleven. Dressed in jeans and a black jacket. We're too far away to see much more than that in this fog."

"Stay with him. We're about two blocks away from the hotel. Call Dopey and tell him to meet us in the lobby. Sleepy and Happy are to remain with Donald Duck."

"This soup is getting thicker, so step it up," Kurt said.

"Donald Duck, Dopey, Sleepy, Happy! That was the most stupid conversation I've ever heard," Trish declared when he slipped the phone back into his pocket. "I hope it was more intelligent on the other end. Do you fellows actually use those ridiculous names? Furthermore, you're mixing up your toons. Donald Duck is Mickey and Minnie's friend. The Seven Dwarfs prefer the company of Snow White. I hope you gave me a name, too, in this game."

"We didn't have time, but I'd recommend Cruella DeVille."

Dave took her elbow and hurried her along. She practically had to run to keep up with him.

Suddenly several thuds slammed into the building beside them.

"Dammit! He's got a silencer!" Dave cursed. He grabbed her hand and they started to run. Another bullet bounced off the sidewalk at their feet.

They ducked into an alley and Dave motioned her to silence. Then he pulled a pistol out from under the leg of his jeans.

Trish's heart was pounding in her chest. She had no idea what this was all about, but trusted Dave and remained silent. It all was too much to try and absorb. Four days ago she was sweltering in the bright sunshine of Washington, D.C. Now she was crouched in a swirling fog in an alley in Germany with Dave Cassidy—the last man she expected to see holding a gun in his hand. This had to be the mother of all nightmares.

They heard the sound of running feet and Dave shoved her lower and raised his weapon. He gave two short whistles when he recognized the two men who came into view.

Kurt Bolen and Justin Addison ducked into the alley and joined them.

"Sorry, Dave, we lost him in the fog," Kurt said.

They made it to the hotel without any further incident. Don Fraser met them in the lobby.

"How long have you been down here?"

"A couple minutes," Don said.

"Anyone come in?"

"Not since I arrived. What's going on?"

"Is Manning okay?"

"Yeah, Pete and Rick are with him. Manning didn't like being pulled away from some *fraülein* he was hitting on at the bar. He's a real piece of work. Am I the only one who can't stand that guy?"

"There's a big fraternity," Dave said. "Let's get upstairs."

After checking out her room, Dave proceeded to give Trish explicit instructions. "Keep the door locked. A couple of us will be outside it all night, so don't worry."

"Are you saying someone is trying to kill me?" Trish asked. "How do you know the man wasn't shooting at you?"

Dave shook his head. "No reason to make me the target. At first I thought it was CIA keeping tabs on you until the shooting started. At this point, we still want to keep you alive."

"Why would anyone want to kill me?" she asked. "I don't even know what this is all about."

"I bet your husband knows. The shooter may have been sending him a message. By the way, stay away from the window. Whoever it was is still out there somewhere."

"Thank you, Agent Cassidy," she grumbled. "I'll try not to keep that thought in mind when I attempt to fall asleep."

Trish soon found out that truer words were never spoken. After several hours of tossing and turning, she finally managed to fall asleep, only to awaken a short while later to a ringing telephone and bright sunlight streaming through the window.

The call was from Justin Addison, who informed her they would be leaving for the airport in thirty minutes.

Trish jumped out of bed, took a quick shower, then dressed in the jogging suit again. She stuffed her other clothes into the paper bag and was ready when the knock sounded on the door.

Robert was with them. It was the first time she'd seen him since they'd arrived at the hotel. If he was aware of it, he didn't mention or make a pretense of showing any concern over the attempt on her life last night.

She'd like to tell him a thing or two. He owed her a big apology—not that he'd ever offer one. But thanks to him she now was the target of an assassin.

While waiting for the plane to be gassed up, Dave came over and handed her a paper cup of hot coffee and a Danish pastry packaged in plastic.

"Sorry, this is the best I could rustle up."

She smiled gratefully. "Thanks." She took a deep draft of the hot brew. It was perfectly sweetened to her taste. She smiled in appreciation. He hadn't forgotten.

A short time later they boarded a cargo plane without any further delay and all of them slept most of the way back to the States.

As soon as they landed at Andrews Air Force Base, they were met by the CIA and taken to a room on the base. Same modus operandi, same questions and the same answers from her. The only difference this time was that her interrogators were a Mr. Baker and Mr. Bishop.

By the time Baker and Bishop had finished questioning her, the squad had dispersed. Robert was also nowhere in sight. A polite driver in a black limo drove her home to Georgetown.

Nothing was as comforting as the sight of home. She had a lot to hash out in her mind, but the physical exhaustion and emotional stress of the last few days had drained all her energy. She'd have to think about it tomorrow.

"Now you know how Scarlet felt, Trish," she murmured.

"I beg your pardon, ma'am," the driver said, offering his hand to assist her out of the car.

"Oh nothing. Nothing at all," she said.

Julie, the maid, and Trish's dog Ayevol greeted her at the door with his usual enthusiasm. The cocker spaniel's wagging tail beat a hearty welcome. She wrote a short note to her father, then took a quick shower and climbed into bed.

Ayevol jumped up on the bed and stretched out with his head on her thigh.

"You won't believe who I've been with the last couple of days," she said, scratching him behind his ears. She rested her hand on the dog's head. "I was with him, Ayevol. I'll tell you all about it tomorrow, sweetheart." She patted the dog on the head. "After all, 'tomorrow is another day.'"

Right on, Miss Scarlet.

With a pleased smile, Trish closed her eyes and slept.

The first thing Trish did when she woke up was reach for the telephone and call Deb. She hadn't spoken to her best friend for a week and could not wait to tell her the news. They agreed to meet for breakfast.

An hour later Trish smiled with pleasure as she watched men's gazes follow the tall, willowy blonde crossing the floor of the restaurant to join her.

The two women had been inseparable companions since childhood, had attended a Swiss boarding school together in their early teens and later had graduated from Wellesley together. Soon after, Deb had married Dr. Thomas Carpenter, ten years her senior and a successful brain surgeon. Two years ago, she and Deb had formed an interior decorating business, which had begun to build up a respected reputation.

"Darling, you are absolutely glowing," Deb said when she sat down. "I know it can't be that you're pregnant, so what is it?"

The salutation was Deb's usual greeting to everyone. It was a convenient affectation that she carried off so well that most people never suspected that often it served a double purpose. Through the years, the greeting had become a signal between them for Trish to recognize by the tone of voice in the way she said it, when Deb either liked or distrusted an individual. This had often proven to be very useful in dealing with people, both socially and in business.

"Deb, you are not going to believe this." With a smug smile, Trish handed Deb a copy of her divorce papers, then sat back and laughed at her friend's reaction as she perused it.

Deb squealed with joy. "The scourge finally signed the divorce papers!" She glanced at Trish askance. "What did you do, hold a gun to his head?"

"Now you know I'm more up close and personal than that," Trish teased. "I held a knife to his throat."

"We've got to celebrate this." Deb motioned to the waiter. "Darling, a couple of Bloody Marys, please."

"Can't we settle for orange juice?"

"Not on your life. Tom and I have been waiting for this day as much as you have. Let's hear all the delicious details."

Trish told her of her agreement to accompany Robert to Morocco. As much as she hated to withhold anything from her friend, she honored her word to the CIA and kept out of the conversation any mention of their involvement or the rescue by a special ops squad.

Deb whipped out her cell phone. "I've got to tell Tom. He'll be ecstatic."

"Hold up. I have something more to tell you. I ran into Dave Cassidy."

Debra's green eyes widened with disbelief. "You're kidding! Where?"

Now what? She hated lying to Deb. "He was on the same plane as we were coming back from Germany." At least that was the truth.

"You mean he came here on business?"

"Apparently he lives here."

Deb threw her hands up in the air. "Tom and I go away for a week, and this is what happens. Is he married?"

"I didn't ask."

"You didn't ask!"

"I noticed he wasn't wearing a wedding ring."

"That doesn't always mean anything. You know some men remove them when their wives aren't around."

"Debra, I'm talking about Dave. Mr. Straight-and-Narrow Cassidy."

"Trish, that doesn't sound like you. When did you become so cynical?"

She sighed. "Yeah, I know. That's how my father contemptuously refers to Dave."

"Henry has his own agenda." Deb reached over and squeezed her hand. "So how did it go?"

"Horribly." Trish looked up desolately. "He's very bitter, Deb. I think he hates me."

"He doesn't hate you, Trish. Good Lord, anyone who ever saw the two of you together knows Dave could never hate you. He's probably carrying the same torch that you are, and when he found out you were married, it probably made matters worse."

"I am not carrying a torch for Dave Cassidy. I just want us to be friends again."

"Right. He's as ugly as sin, as mean as a junkyard dog and could never function below the waist, anyway. I'm glad we've got that settled. However, darling, having said that, I question if you read his body language correctly. Dave more likely is more jealous than bitter. And if that's the case, it's a darn better sign he's not married than the fact that he wasn't wearing a wedding ring."

"Easy for you to say," Trish murmured and lowered her head in dejection.

"Did you tell him you're a free woman now?"

"That would have been difficult to explain since I was with Robert. Besides, I think I'd be wasting my time. He clearly is not interested in having me in his life."

"You'll never know unless you try. Don't you know by now, darling, men don't understand the game of love. They go blundering through it like storm troopers. It always takes the right woman to explain it to them."

Laughing, the two women clinked their glasses. "Men," they said in unison.

"Hey, what is that?" Trish reached over and grabbed Deb's wrist. "New, isn't it?" she asked, staring at the diamond and gold bracelet on Deb's wrist. "Did you and Tom raid Tiffany's when you were in New York?"

"Just a little bauble Tom gave me for our eighth wedding anniversary," Deb replied, tongue-in-cheek. "Cute, isn't it?"

"Oh, yes. *Cute,* Deb. There are enough diamonds there to…" Diamonds. She suddenly remembered Colin McDermott had mentioned diamonds to Robert in Morocco.

"To what?" Deb asked.

Trish snapped back to awareness. "I'm sorry, what did you say?"

"You were saying there are enough diamonds to what?"

"To blind a person, Debra Carpenter. Shame on you."

Deb took a long look at the bracelet. "There are a lot, aren't there?"

"I'll say. It must have cost a mint."

Deb's smooth brow creased in a frown. "You don't suppose Tom is having an affair, do you?"

"Yeah, right!" Trish scoffed. "When mules fly like Pegasus."

The two women looked at each other, broke into laughter, and once again clinked their glasses together.

As soon as Trish returned home, she looked up the telephone number of Kim Harrington in New York, and was lucky enough to catch her at home. In loyalty to her brother, Kim refused to give her Dave's address. After Trish explained they had run into each other again, and she had to talk to him, Kim finally conceded that at age thirty-four her big brother was old enough to handle his own problems. She relented and gave Trish Dave's telephone number and address.

Thoughts about McDermott, Robert and diamonds kept running through Trish's mind for the rest of the day. She had forgotten about the diamonds entirely and realized she had never mentioned them to the CIA. From what she remembered of the conversation between Robert and McDermott, the Irishman had indicated Robert had the diamonds in his possession. He would still have to have them because he and Ali had never left her before Dave and his squad showed up. And since they'd been transported home on military planes, Robert could easily have smuggled the diamonds into the country. She was curious enough to try and find out.

Trish rooted hurriedly through a dresser drawer, found what she was looking for, and hurried back to her car.

Chapter 4

From habit Dave glanced around the barroom as soon as he entered. The place had begun to fill with the after-work crowd. Singles hoping to make a lucky connection for the night and tired businessmen needing a jolt of whiskey to jump-start their psyches and get back in the race.

He walked over to the bar, sat down on one of the stools and ordered a Scotch on the rocks.

He'd finished the drink and was nursing the second one by the time Mike Bishop showed up and slipped onto the stool beside him.

"Sorry I'm late. Baker caught me on my way out." Mike ordered a beer and as soon as the bartender left, he asked, "So, what's on your mind, Dave?"

"Prince Charming's not too happy with me these days," Dave said, referring to Jeff Baker's code name in the Agency. "I figure it's because of the mission."

"That's bullshit, Dave. Nobody's blaming you. This isn't the first mission that went bad. Hell, I can think of a dozen or more of them when I was leading the squad."

"He says the Agency's taking heat over the bin Muzzar slaying. Mike, I swear my squad had nothing to do with his death. We didn't fire a shot until we reached the cover of the rocks. If he was killed at the palace, it was after we pulled out."

"I believe you and so does Baker. And we all knew the whole damn mission stunk from the beginning. You gotta let it go, Dave."

Dave motioned to the bartender for a refill. "What about McDermott? I want another crack at him, Mike."

"You'll get it. That is if the Brits don't get to him first. They've got their own ax to grind with him. Right now, no one knows where he is. He's got a slew of aliases and fake passports. The SOB could be anywhere. It's going to take time to track him down, but I promise you the Dwarf Squad will get the call when we do."

"You get anything of value out of his backpack?"

"Just another alias and a phony passport."

"I gather you didn't get anything out of Manning either."

"No. Claims he never met the guy until then."

"Yeah, right."

Dave shrugged. "What can I say? His wife gave us the same story. She came across pretty sincere to me, but she could be a damn good actress."

"Yeah, a guy's a fool to believe anything a woman tells him." Dave picked up his drink and downed it. "What?" he asked in response to Mike's puzzled stare.

"You're beginning to sound like me before I met Ann. What's your problem, Dave?"

"Colin McDermott. That's my problem."

"Screw McDermott. How come you're suddenly belting down shots of Scotch like they're lemonade? You want to talk about it?"

"I'll get around to it sometime. I'm just not ready right now. Like I'll ever be. Right now I'm so screwed up, I can't even think straight."

"Well, when you are, you know my number."

For the next quarter hour they discussed whether the Packers would beat the Redskins on Sunday, then Mike finished his drink and stood up.

"I've got to get going. This is Lamaze night."

Dave shook his head. "Who'd have ever believed it? You're really eating up married life, aren't you?"

"You've got that right. Every bite of it, pal. Ann's the best thing that's ever happened to me. I'm one lucky bastard, Dave, and I know it."

"Do you ever miss it, Mike?"

"Miss what?"

"Missions. The rush."

"Hell, no! I was fed up with that life before I even met Ann. She's shown me how good life can really be. It's time *you* ought to think about settling down and starting a family."

"What is it about you married guys? Once you lose your freedom, you don't rest until you take your friends down with you. Misery loves company, is that it?"

Mike chuckled. "You're right about one thing, Dave. Marriage *is* real misery—when I'm away from Ann. What gets me through the day most of the time is knowing she and Brandon will be at home waiting for me."

Mike finished his drink. "Speaking of sharing your life, pal, looks like you can have some company of your own tonight, if you're interested. That blonde down there can't keep her eyes off you."

Dave glanced at the attractive woman sitting alone at the end of the bar. She smiled at him.

"I'll leave you to finer pursuits." Mike slapped him on the shoulder. "No time like the present. Go for it, pal. I'll see you in the morning."

The bartender came over with the bottle of Scotch. "Ready for another, Dave?"

He nodded. "What's the lady drinking, Bernie?"

"Chardonnay."

"Give her a refill."

He watched Bernie amble down to the other end of the bar and fill the woman's glass. They exchanged a few words and then she nodded toward Dave, picked up the glass and smiled again at him.

Dave stood up and reached for his glass. Nodding at the blonde, he raised it in a slight toast. Then he killed the Scotch, tossed some bills on the bar and left the barroom.

He was in no mood to make a connection. Lord knows he needed one. Seeing Trish again had tied him in knots. Knots the blonde wouldn't be able to free, any better than any other women had in the past six years. They'd all been nothing but a necessary physical release and emotion never entered into the act.

When in hell would it end? It had been six years now. When would he be able to look at a woman and want her as much as he'd always wanted Trish every time he saw her? As much as he wanted her right now even knowing she was a married woman—knowing what she had become.

Looking back now, he realized his dad had been the same way. Even though his mom had died young, his dad had never considered remarrying. Dave couldn't recall his dad even dating another woman—much less bringing one home. What about his needs? Female companionship. Sex. Was it like this for him, too?

The realization filled him with shame. He had never thought about his father's needs while he was growing up. In fact, he and his sister had taken pride in knowing their dad had gone to his grave never loving any other woman but their mother. What selfish self-indulgence on their parts!

"Forgive me, Dad. Guess I deserve what I'm getting. I understand now what you must have gone through, but it's too late to tell you."

Pausing outside the bar, Dave took a deep breath. The fresh air felt good. The four drinks had begun to hit him, so he decided to hike the three miles to his apartment in the hope of walking off the effects of the alcohol.

Dammit! Seeing Trish again—and what she had become—dredged up memories he'd rather forget. He had good cause to get drunk—and stay that way—but he'd be damned if he'd start falling into bed at night in a drunken stupor.

He turned and strode down the block.

Trish felt a stab of pain the instant she saw Dave coming down the block. She'd recognize the shape of his head anywhere, the broad outline of his shoulders and the easy grace with which he moved through any crowd.

She'd been sitting in her car for the past hour waiting for him. Thank God he was alone. She would have driven away if he hadn't been.

Her gaze fixed lovingly on his tall figure as she watched him enter the building and pause at the bank of mailboxes.

As he checked his mail, the firm features of his profile were spotlighted in the lobby's brightness. Nothing appeared to have changed in six years. The same tanned face with its straight nose, sensual mouth and square jaw. He still wore his dark hair neatly clipped to his proud head. If anything, he was more handsome. Her heart ached looking at him. Would she ever get over this man?

She waited as he disappeared through the inner door. Shortly after, a light went on in a front apartment on the second floor.

Her courage began to falter again. What was she doing coming here? A dozen or more times in the past hour she had waged an inner struggle to turn on the ignition of her car and drive away as quickly as she could.

Before she could lose her nerve again, Trish got out of the car and crossed the street. The building was not secure, and she entered the inner door and started to climb the stairs to the second floor. Each step she took was like plucking the petals off a daisy—Should I go? Should I stay? Recalling the loathing in his eyes made it hopeless to ponder "he loves me, he loves me not." He loved her not! So what had possessed her to come here?

She paused outside the door marked 2A.

Dave had just tossed aside his suit jacket and loosened his tie when a knock sounded on the door. It had to be Mrs. Graham from across the hall. What was her problem now?

Three years ago he had prevented her from being mugged and since then, whenever he was home, she had him doing odds-and-ends jobs, from loosening jar covers to taking care of her cat when she went out of town. Not only did he hate cats—their dander made him sneeze—but he was always on call. The squad could be sent out on an hour's notice at all times.

Besides, if he wanted the responsibility of a pet, he'd have his own. He loved dogs. The vision of Ayevol, the buff-colored cocker spaniel he and Trish had had when they were together, flashed through his mind in a painful memory. He sure missed that little hound.

Nevertheless, as much a nuisance as Mrs. Graham could be, she was a sweet old lady and he never had the heart to turn her down. In addition, she kept him supplied with the best homemade chocolate chip cookies he'd ever tasted.

Anticipating her holding a plate of them, he smiled and opened the door.

"What can I do for you, Mrs.—" The words froze in his throat.

Don't do this to me, God.

"Hello, Dave. May I come in? I have to talk to you."

"I don't think that would be wise, Mrs. Manning. Besides, I can't think of anything we have to say to each other."

"It's very important, Dave."

He turned away. She followed him in and gently closed the door. Then she hesitated as if she was drawing strength from the feel of the solid wood.

Dave folded his arms across his chest and leaned against the wall. "So what's so important, Mrs. Manning?"

"Do you mind if I sit down?"

"Does it matter? You usually do what you want anyway."

He could see she was trembling. He wasn't in the best condition himself. The walk and night air had worked off most of the Scotch, but he still was in no condition for a face-off with her.

"Sorry, I only have beer or Scotch to offer you. If I

remember, your tastes run toward white wine. Of course, that was six years ago. It would appear that many of your tastes have changed since then."

"I don't want anything to drink. I need someone's advice."

"Daddy out of town?"

She flinched at the sarcasm. "Please, Dave, let's not throw darts at each other."

So what if the remark was childish and spiteful? Thanks to her he had stored up six years of bitterness and resentment. It was about time he got some of it off his chest.

"So what's so important? Say what you came to say and get out of here."

She bolted to her feet and headed for the door. "I can see this was a mistake." She paused at the door and looked back accusingly.

"You used to be a nice guy, Dave. I'm sorry I bothered you." She turned again to depart.

"That's the kettle calling the pot black."

She spun on her heel. "What is that supposed to mean?"

"You've got a short memory, lady. Have you forgotten we walked in on that ménage à trois you were about to enjoy. Or were you too drunk to remember?"

"You don't understand. That was happening against my will. I couldn't stop them."

"Yeah, right. And you weren't stinking drunk either. They drugged you. Right? Look, Mrs. Manning, whatever bedroom games you and your husband like to play is not my business."

"It's true. They did drug me," she cried out.

"You said you had something important to tell me. Does it relate to Colin McDermott?"

"I think Robert is mixed up in some kind of crooked operation with McDermott and bin Muzzar."

He snorted. "Gee, you don't say."

"Forget it."

She opened the door to leave. He was being stupid. Letting his emotions cloud his common sense. Maybe she did know something that could help the Agency and it would be prudent for him to listen to her.

"Okay. Okay. Relax. Let's hear it."

She closed the door and came back and sat down. "If you don't mind, I will have something to drink. A glass of water will be fine."

A half wall separated the living room from the kitchen. Trish watched him as he got an ice tray out of the freezer. She could envision the play of muscles across his shoulders as he worked at releasing the cubes and yearned to go up behind him and slip her arms around his waist, cuddle against him and lay her head against his back the way she had done so often when they were together.

"How long have you lived here, Dave?"

."Came back to D.C. about three years ago."

Three years. She'd still been single three years ago. If only she'd known. If only…

He came back and handed her the glass of water. "You still living in that apartment we had?"

"No. I moved back home shortly after I married Robert."

"When did you get married?"

"Two years ago."

"Two years." Remorse flickered in his eyes. For a long moment their gazes locked, and she wondered if he was thinking the same thoughts she was. Then he walked away and leaned against the wall again.

"So what is it you came to say?"

Trish took a drink of the water and then put the glass aside.

"I don't know if there's anything to this. It very well could be entirely innocent, but nevertheless certainly unusual. I remembered Mr. McDermott saying something about diamonds to Robert and Ali." She paused, waiting for him to absorb what she had just told him.

"And…?"

"It appeared he expected some kind of exchange for them. Robert implied he hadn't had time to examine them yet. Thinking about it, I can't imagine why Robert would even be interested in diamonds."

"I'm sure you're in a better position to judge that than I am."

"Robert works for my father. He's a banker, not a gem dealer."

"Did you mention this to the Agency?"

"I'd forgotten about it until today. When I remembered, I thought it might be worth pursuing. Since I still had my key to the apartment, I went back there and waited until Robert left. Then I went inside and checked the contents in the safe. I discovered a pouch of uncut diamonds."

"Why would he put a pouch of diamonds in a place where you could discover them so easily?"

"I told you why. I'm not living with him. I haven't seen or talked to him since our return yesterday. We have nothing to do with each other. I moved in with my father more than a year and a half ago. We had signed divorce papers before we went to North Africa."

He didn't even blink, but just continued to look at her with an inscrutable expression.

"If that's the case, why did you even go to North Africa with him?"

"He refused to give me a divorce unless I did."

"So you're implying he acquired the diamonds during the trip?"

"I don't know. Maybe he did have them before. I'm only saying diamonds were mentioned in his conversation with McDermott. And Robert had a pouch of uncut diamonds in his safe. That sounds pretty coincidental to me."

"This should be bounced off Baker and Bishop. Why come to me?"

"To get your advice. You work for them."

"But it's not my field. I'm part of a special operations squad, Mrs. Manning. I don't work at the Agency's think tank. You need to take this information to those guys."

"Very well. I'll contact them in the morning." She got up and moved to the door. "Thank you for listening."

"I'll call a cab for you."

"That's not necessary. I drove here."

"Then I'll walk you to your car."

As they left, a woman carrying a cat came out of the apartment across the hall from him.

"Hello, David. I'm glad to see you're back home."

"Glad to be back, Mrs. Graham," he said. Her inquisitive look swept over Trish, but Dave did not introduce them.

He was silent as they went downstairs, crossed the street and opened the car door.

"I suggest you get in touch with Mike Bishop first thing in the morning."

Trish slid behind the wheel. "I will. Thank you, Dave. I'm sorry I bothered you with this."

"By the way, I'm not in the phone book. How did you know where to find me?"

She should have expected the question, but it caught

her off guard. "I...uh...don't remember. I must have got it from the CIA."

"Like hell you did. They don't give out agents' addresses."

"Very well, if you must know, your sister told me."

"Women!" he grumbled, feeling betrayed. "You can't trust any of them."

He slammed the car door and walked away. His head was pounding and his insides churning. Every inch of him throbbed from his need for her; his fingers still tingled from wanting to touch her; and the scent of her still teased his nostrils.

Dammit! She had no right to show up here tonight. Her nearness, the sound of her voice, those beautiful blue eyes sheathed in anguish ripping at his guts.

It was the damn Scotch he'd drunk that was doing this to him. Nothing was more pathetic than a self-pitying drunk crying the blues.

He finished undressing and climbed into the shower in the hope of clearing his head.

Dave closed his eyes and lifted his face toward the spray. If only the pelting water could cleanse the image of Trish from his mind. Instead each drop felt like a needle prick, a painful reminder of the last time they had showered together.

He had the mother of all headaches. His head felt too heavy to hold up. He didn't look forward to what lay ahead and was trying to figure out what to say when the shower door suddenly opened and Trish stood there wearing only a grin and a pixie gleam in those gorgeous blue eyes.

"Hi, cowboy. Room for one more?"

He opened his arms. "What do you think, angel?"

She stepped into the stall and slipped her arms around his neck. "So, how was your day?"

It sure as hell would get worse with what he had to tell her; but at the moment, with the feel of her pressed against him, it was about to become a damn sight better.

Her water-slickened body curved into his as he kissed her hungrily.

She felt so good. Her skin was warm and wet. He moved his fingers across the sleek satin of her shoulders and down to the hollow of her spine. Grasping the rounded cheeks in his hands, he lifted her up and she curled her legs around his hips.

She groaned with arousal, searching for his mouth. She found it and her tongue worked his as their moistened bodies adhered to each other, the taut nipples of her breasts a sweet piercing against his chest. He raised her higher until he could get his mouth on them, then he suckled.

Moaning with ecstasy, she threw back her head. Blood pounded at his temples and his organ felt on fire. He had to climax or he'd implode.

"Angel, I'm on the edge of blasting off. Please tell me you're ready."

"I was ready before I came in here," she murmured.

It was the kind of remark from her that always sent his testosterone into overdrive. He drove into her and she tightened around him. The rapturous body rhythm began, escalating faster and faster. Intensifying as it sucked the breath out of both of them in the mindlessness that led to that final explosive release as she cried out his name.

She always cried out his name when she climaxed. That was another thing about her that always turned him right back on.

The spray continued to rain down on them. He made no attempt to pull out or let her down. She slumped her head against his chest and he held her as his breathing slowly returned to normal.

Only then did he lower her, but she remained cuddled against him in the circle of his arms. Once again his mouth and hands sought the feel and taste of her. He pressed a light kiss to her shoulder, then ran his fingers down her back and played with her spine. He knew if he kept it up, it would lead to another arousal.

She felt too good to stop.

"What are you thinking about?" he asked.

She raised her head and looked up at him. "How much I love you."

"I love you, too, angel. No one knows how I love you!" His mouth explored the soft hollow of her neck.

She stepped away. "I think we'd better get out of this shower before we pucker up like a couple of prunes."

"Plums. Plums pucker into prunes. Besides, they're round and juicy. I'd rather visualize you as a plum." He lowered his head and laved at the water clinging to the nipples of her breasts, then closed his mouth around the turgid peak of one of them.

"Yes, definitely round and juicy."

"I can see where this is leading," she said. "We've got to get out of here and get dressed. Did you forget my dad's expecting us for dinner?" She stepped out of the shower, grabbed a towel, and headed for the bedroom.

Dave turned off the water and for a long moment stared at the glossy black shower tiles. Show time. No putting it off any longer.

He dried off, wrapped a towel around his waist, and went into the bedroom. Trish had already slipped into a white blouse and black slacks. His gaze fixed on her. She was so beautiful. He wanted to reach for her again.

"Hey, will you get the lead out, my love. You know Dad doesn't like us to be late." She came over and kissed him lightly on the cheek, then sat down at the vanity and began to brush out her hair.

"I'm not going to your father's for dinner. Trish, I resigned today."

She giggled. "I know these Wednesday-night dinners don't thrill you, but resign yourself back to grin-and-bear-them."

"I resigned from the firm, Trish."

She spun around on the stool. "What are you talking about?" The laughter in her eyes had shifted to shock.

"I'd like to get as far away from this town as I can. Let's fly to Vegas, get married, and then I'll contact a headhunter."

She got to her feet. "What's this all about, Dave? Did you and Dad have an argument?"

"Yeah, one hell of a one."

She came over and slipped her arms around his waist. "Sweetheart, I know there's a lot of tension between you and Dad since we set up housekeeping together, but once we're married, he'll get over it."

"That's not the issue, Trish."

"Then what is? Why are you considering leaving the firm?"

"It's not up for consideration, Trish. I left the firm."

"Why?"

He knew from the tilt of her chin that her guard was up and the argument had begun.

"I think it would be wiser to get the explanation from your father."

"In as much as you happen to be the man I love and intend to marry, I think I'm not unreasonable to expect an explanation from you."

"No, it's not unreasonable," he said.

What the hell was he doing standing there with only a damn towel around his waist trying to explain a problem that could affect their relationship—and probably break her heart. He grabbed a pair of shorts out of the drawer and pulled them on. They neither restored his dignity nor bolstered his courage.

"You know how much I love you, angel. And that I would never deliberately try to hurt you."

He could see he was getting through to her. That earlier impatient gleam in her eyes had changed into one of apprehension.

"And I love you, too, Dave. So what is this all about?"

"Today I happened to notice a suspicious pattern in a Syrian account that had been opened and handled exclusively by your father. Every deposit made by them was immediately transferred to a company in Belfast, Ireland."

"So maybe this Irish company is a subsidiary of the Syrian corporation."

"That was my initial thought until I read further. Our files indicated that these transfers were funds being paid to the Irish company for the purchase of ball bearings. I wondered, why bother to come through us rather than deal directly with each other? It reeked to high heaven to me. I did some checking and discovered the Irish company didn't even manufacture the item being purchased. It's a clear case of money laundering. The company had to be just a front for the IRA."

"I don't understand. Are you referring to the Irish Republican Army?"

"*Exactly. The whole thing is an ongoing money-laundering set-up to finance them.*"

For a long moment she appeared confused, then her eyes widened as it all began to sink in. "*Did you tell my father about this?*"

"*Of course. As soon as I found out myself.*"

"*And what did he say?*"

"*He told me it was not my concern, and to keep my nose out of his personal accounts.*"

"*And that's what led to the argument between the two of you.*" *He nodded. She sighed in relief.* "*You know Dad has a short fuse. By tomorrow it will all be forgotten.*"

"*Trish, don't you understand? Your father's involved in a money-laundering scheme that's funding Irish terrorists.*"

"*You don't know if he was aware of what was happening.*"

"*Of course he knew.*"

"*You don't know that,*" *she lashed out.* "*How dare you accuse him of being dishonest. No wonder he was angry with you.*"

"*Good Lord, Trish. How naive can you be? Your father's in it up to his eyeballs. Why do you think he personally handles the accounts? Any other guy in the office would have seen through it as quickly as I did.*"

"*You're jumping to conclusions. Why are you doing this, Dave? I know you and Dad have this tug-of-war over me, but I didn't believe you disliked him so much that you'd accuse him of being unethical.*"

Tears glistened in her eyes and he reached out to embrace her. She shoved his hands away.

"*My father's a good and honest man. Do you have any idea how much you've hurt me with your accusa-*

tions about a man I love dearly? He raised and cared for me all my life." Sobbing openly, she turned away.

Dave couldn't bear witnessing her heartache. He moved to her and attempted to draw her back into his arms.

"Don't touch me. I'll never forgive you for this. You're trying to force me to choose between the two of you."

"And you're trying to force me to surrender my integrity and ignore what he's done. If I did, it would eventually destroy our love."

"He's my father, Dave. I can't..." She was sobbing so hard she couldn't continue, but her next action spoke louder than the words she couldn't impart. She slid the ring off her finger and put it on the vanity. Then she grabbed her purse, called to their cocker spaniel and ran out with him.

He held out hope that she would cool down and come to her senses, but when she hadn't returned by midnight he knew she wasn't coming back.

Dave paced the floor throughout the night, cursing himself for losing the only person who mattered to him.

In the morning he packed up his belongings and walked away from the whole stinking mess.

Dave turned off the shower and grasped the metal showerhead as if it were a lifeline. The weight in his chest felt like a vise squeezing the breath out of him. Somehow he had to exorcise that woman from his mind and heart.

Chapter 5

After driving aimlessly around D.C., Trish found herself near the Ellipse. Since it was a pleasant night and the streets were well populated, she parked her car and sat down on a bench near the Lincoln Monument.

She wouldn't allow herself to cry. Even if she had to choke on her tears, she wouldn't shed one of them. She wasn't worthy of even self-pity. How could one woman be so stupid so many times in the same lifetime? She'd been on top of the world—and she'd let that happiness slip through her fingers.

It had been a big mistake to go and see Dave tonight. Only one of many mistakes she'd made in the past six years. She didn't know which one was worse: walking out on Dave six years ago or marrying Robert Manning.

And now, knowing Dave was so near, how could she stay away from him? She'd seen the contempt in his eyes tonight. How could she ever convince him he was wrong? That she hadn't done any of those things he'd accused her of doing.

Trish had no idea how long she sat struggling with the agonizing thoughts before she became aware that the streams of tourists viewing the monument had begun to thin. In a state of rejection, she returned to her car and drove home.

She pulled into the driveway of her father's house in Georgetown. In this exclusive D.C. neighborhood the cost of houses ranged in the millions. She parked her car in the garage. As she walked toward the front door, somehow, despite the distraction of her disturbing thoughts, she began to feel that someone was watching her. She swung her head toward a rustle in the shrubbery lining the walk.

"Hello, is someone there?"

When there was no reply, she moved on, but quickened her step. She was too edgy. The events of the last couple days had frayed her nerves.

Suddenly she heard the distinct sound of rustling again. Trish spun on her heel. "Who's there?"

She sighed in relief when a blond cocker spaniel came out of the bushes and trotted over to her.

"Ayevol! You scared the life out of me!" She knelt down and the dog lapped at her cheek as she scratched it behind the ears. "What are you doing out here alone?"

Ayevol scampered ahead of her, and to her further surprise she found the front door ajar. "So that's how you got outside," she declared. "Who left the door open?"

The foyer was brightly lit and Trish closed and locked the door. She decided to tell her father about the diamonds. His den was in darkness, so she proceeded to the kitchen. Only a night-light burned there. The whole situation was beginning to work on her already tattered nerves.

Ayevol scampered up the stairway ahead of her. She was relieved to see light shining from her father's room at the end of the hallway. She tapped lightly on the open door and entered.

"Dad, I have to talk to you." Her father was standing at the bathroom sink.

"What happened?" she asked when he came out holding a wet washcloth to his forehead.

His light laughter diminished her alarm. "Would you believe I walked into a door?"

"Let me look at it."

He sat down on the edge of the bed and Trish examined the wound. The skin wasn't broken, but a good-size bruise had already discolored a spot on his tanned forehead. "Maybe you should have a doctor check you out."

"Nonsense! I'm fine." He got up hastily and returned to examine his face in the mirror.

Trish's gaze remained fixed fondly on him. The years had done little to diminish his handsomeness. Tall, with a full head of gray hair and a well-conditioned body, at age fifty-five he was still considered to be one of the most eligible bachelors in D.C., a city that overflowed with wealthy, good-looking, ivy-league competition.

Driven by ambition, despite being orphaned as a child, he had worked his way through college, studied hard to learn his chosen profession and become one of the most successful international bankers in Washington. He had also managed to ingratiate himself as a favorite of many of the self-made nouveau riche of the city.

Trish adored her father. She'd been only five years old when her mother had died in an airplane accident.

He became the most important thing in her life. Trish had centered all her love and attention on him. In return, Henry had spoiled and lavished her with luxuries, expensive clothes and the finest education money could buy in the years that followed.

In outward appearances her life seemed perfect, but Trish had always had a nagging feeling that something was lacking.

Until two years ago, when she had gone into business with Deb, Trish had felt her life was too idle. The volunteer and charity work she did was not enough to satisfy her. From the time she had left college, her father had preferred she continue to devote her time and attention to running his home and standing in as his official hostess.

But her life had seemed to her to hold no real purpose until the day he introduced her to Dave Cassidy, a brilliant young executive her father had recently hired. Talk along the grapevine was that Cassidy would either be running Hunter International or his own business within a few years.

She and Dave had fallen in love instantly, and for the first time in her twenty-four years she'd acted in defiance of her father's wishes. Despite her father's disapproval, she moved in with Dave. A month later Dave asked her to marry him, and six months after that her enchanted world spun out of orbit and came crashing to a halt.

Her heart was broken when the two men she loved had clashed. Out of loyalty to the man who had raised her, she had taken her father's side. It had led to the break-up between her and Dave.

Despite this, she had never blamed her father—nor Dave. She blamed herself for acting so hastily and not discussing it calmly with Dave. Instead, she had fought with him and broken their engagement. She grimaced in despair. Now at thirty, she had paid a heavy price for that impetuousness.

Recalling the scene with Dave earlier, Trish closed her eyes in anguish.

A price you have to live with the rest of your life, Trish.

"What's wrong, baby?"

Trish opened her eyes and discovered her father was staring at her. "Nothing."

"You said you wanted to talk."

She was no longer in the mood to talk about anything. She would probably end up breaking down if she tried. She needed to be alone.

"Nothing important, Dad. Did you know you left the front door open? Ayevol got out."

"That was careless of me. No harm done, I hope."

"No. No harm done. Good night, Dad."

"Good night, baby."

Returning to her room, Trish drew a hot bath and sat listlessly in the tub as the hot jets bombarded her body, and her mind swirled with even steamier thoughts of Dave.

Early the next morning she dressed, then called the CIA and then hurried downstairs after the call.

After several minutes of nervous pacing, Trish glanced out the window and saw a car coming up the driveway. She quickly grabbed her purse and went outside before her father saw her.

She was in no mood to explain what she intended to do. He would only insist she talk to Robert before going to the CIA. He would probably go straight to Robert with her suspicions, as he'd done so often in the past.

Her father had actually believed that accompanying

Robert to Morocco meant that they were getting back together again. When she'd told him yesterday that they had signed divorce papers before they'd even left, he had stormed out of the room.

As much as she loved her father, she could no longer tolerate the excuses he always offered in Robert's defense. Trish could only wonder what her father would say if she had told him about the drugging and the little party Robert and Ali had planned.

A shudder rippled her spine as she recalled that horrendous scene. Thanks to the timely arrival of Dave's squad, it had all worked out in her favor. Now she had what she wanted—signed divorce papers. Robert Manning would be out of her life once and for all. And she had done it without her father's help.

She hurried up to the car, then drew up in surprise when she recognized the driver.

"Good morning," she said, climbing in.

"Good morning," Dave Cassidy replied, and shifted the car into drive.

"I'm sorry. When I spoke to Mr. Bishop, he told me he'd send a driver for me. It never occurred to me it would be you."

"I've never told Bishop we have a history."

"Maybe you should."

"I can't see why it would be germane to the case, Mrs. Manning. It's ancient history."

"Perhaps so, but at least it might prevent awkward moments like this."

"Suck it up, lady, and live with it."

And that's exactly what she did. She took a deep breath to try and calm her churning stomach, then gazed out the window. They didn't speak another word to each other the rest of the trip.

Trish had never seen the headquarters of the CIA before in Langley, Virginia. It was very impressive. Spread out on 140 acres, the buildings and surrounding grounds could have passed for the campus of a small college.

Dave turned her over to a woman who had her photographed and pinned with a visitor pass, then he escorted her to Jeff Baker's office. Mike Bishop was there, and the two men rose to their feet when she and Dave entered.

"A pleasure to see you again, Mrs. Manning," Baker said. "You remember Mr. Bishop."

"Yes, of course."

Mike Bishop nodded at her, and then motioned to a chair Dave drew up for her. "Good morning, Mrs. Manning. Please sit down."

"Sir, will it be necessary for me to remain?" Dave asked. "I have some paperwork to go over."

"I'd like you to, Agent Cassidy," Baker said. "This shouldn't take long."

Dave walked over and leaned back against the wall. Trish could tell he didn't like even being in the same room with her. The tension between them was so acute surely the other two men would notice it.

"Let's get right to the point, Mrs. Manning," Baker said. "Mr. Bishop said you recalled a conversation in Morocco regarding diamonds."

With the three men's gazes fixed on her, she began to lose some of her previous confidence. Maybe she was crying wolf and wasting their time.

Her mouth felt dry as she repeated what she had told Dave. As she spoke, she shifted her eyes between Baker and Bishop, deliberately avoiding any eye contact with Dave. But she could feel his stare boring into her. The other men's fixed stares remained on her, their expressions as inscrutable as Dave's had been last night.

"Do you have these diamonds in your possession now, Mrs. Manning?" Baker asked.

"No, sir. I really had no right to be there, much less remove anything from the safe."

"Why is that, Mrs. Manning?"

"I live with my father. Robert Manning and I recently signed divorce papers," she said after a moment.

More men trying to manipulate her. She'd had enough of it and stood up. "For whatever it's worth, gentlemen, that's all I know."

The two men rose to their feet. "Thank you," Baker said. "We appreciate your cooperation, Mrs. Manning."

He picked up a phone, said a few words into it, and then hung up. "I've arranged for your transportation back to D.C. Agent Cassidy, will you see Mrs. Manning to the lobby?"

Once she and Dave were in the elevator, Trish let her disgruntlement be known.

"Will you kindly explain what bringing me way out here has accomplished, that couldn't have been done by telephone?"

"This makes your story official, Mrs. Manning," he said.

She didn't know what was more exasperating: his officiousness or his continuing to call her Mrs. Manning.

"For God's sake, Dave, will you stop addressing me as if we're strangers," she riled in frustration.

"We *are* strangers, Mrs. Manning."

The elevator door swished open and they stepped into the lobby. Outside a black limousine pulled up, and Dave opened the door for her. Trish climbed in and he closed the door.

He didn't say goodbye.

She fumed about it all the way home. The man was

acting like a petulant child. No matter how bitter one might be, there's no excuse for not offering a civil good-bye. Even the limo driver did that, and he didn't even know her!

Trish changed into shorts and a halter and took Ayevol outside to exercise him. She tossed a Frisbee to him until the dog had had enough and went back to his favorite pastime—sniffing at the grass and flowers.

Trish sat down on a bench. Her mind was still struggling with disturbing thoughts.

"You know, Ayevol, it all boils down to the problem of men," she said to the dog, who had settled down at her feet.

"With the exception of you, sweetheart, the male animal is the most immature and confusing creature on earth. They complicate and usually foul up even the simplest acts of daily existence.

"Take my experience with them as an example. Now Deb and I are two females who have been friends since childhood. Our relationship is true and tried. No question about it, we'll be friends for life. Agree?"

She looked down at the dog for reassurance. Ayevol's adoring stare gave her the assurance she sought.

"Now let's analyze the men in my life. My father. He knows I love him dearly, that I respect him and am proud of him. Yet, he insists upon continuing to try and dominate and control me. And in doing so he's succeeded in driving me away and complicating both our lives.

"Lets look at Robert Manning, the man I married. Handsome, charming—could probably be successful at anything he chose to be. So he chose to become a moral degenerate—and there's no question he's very successful at it.

"But why did he choose that? Because somehow and

someway men have to complicate their lives by challenging themselves. No matter what they sink to. Agree?"

Once again she sought and received assurance from the dog. This time in the form of a wagging tail.

"Now, Ayevol, let's analyze those two CIA officials this morning. They already knew the answers to the questions they asked me. So why did they ask them? Why did they drag me way out to Langley, Virginia?

"I'll tell you why. Because men have to play games. Whether it's resorting to subterfuge or passing a football, men have to be the captain of the team, and usually at the expense of the women whose lives are complicated by their actions.

"Which brings me to the issue of Dave Cassidy."

At the mention of Dave's name, Ayevol jumped to his feet and began wagging his rear end so vigorously that it threatened to detach.

"Calm down, sweetheart. I know you're very fond of him. Which, I might add, reflects a certain degree of blind devotion on your part that can only lead to a complication in your life.

"Mr. Phi Betta Kappa is supposedly an intelligent man. At least that is what all his diplomas would indicate. Educated, yes. But intelligent? No. You know why? It takes common sense to be intelligent. He's complicated his life by abandoning common sense and acting like an overgrown, pouting child."

She jumped to her feet. "A big kid who doesn't even have the courtesy to say good-bye."

"I'll get it," she yelled to Julie when the doorbell rang a short time later. She opened the door and two men stood there. Neither man bore even a remote resem-

blance to Jerry Orbach, but she had watched enough
Law and Order episodes to recognize a plainclothes detective when she saw one.

"May I help you?"

They flashed their shields. "Ma'am, I'm Detective
MacPherson and this is my partner, Detective Brady.
We were told we could find a Patricia Manning here."

"I'm Patricia Manning. What do you want?"

"I'm afraid we have some bad news, ma'am."

Her heart began pounding in her chest. "Has something happened to my father?"

"May we come in, ma'am?" MacPherson said.

Trish stepped aside and they stepped in. "Please,
what is it? Is my father okay?"

MacPherson shook his head. "This concerns your
husband, Robert Manning."

Trish felt overwhelmed with relief. She took a deep
breath to try and slow her breathing. "What has he
done now?"

The two detectives exchanged glances. "When was
the last time you saw or spoke to your husband, Mrs.
Manning?"

"The day before yesterday at the airport."

"So you had no contact with him yesterday?"

"No. We don't live together. Robert and I recently
divorced."

"Was it an amicable divorce, Mrs. Manning?"

"Anything but," she replied candidly.

The two detectives exchanged meaningful glances
again. It was such a male thing that she wanted to
scream with impatience.

"Just what is this all about, Detective? If some woman has filed a complaint against him, hooray for her. But
it is no concern of mine, so kindly keep me out of it."

"No, ma'am, that's not why we're here," MacPherson said. "Mrs. Manning, we would like you to come with us to the morgue. We have a body that has tentatively been identified as Robert Manning. We would like you to make an official identification."

"Robert is dead? What happened? Was it an accident?"

"No, ma'am. It was a homicide."

"A homicide!" The news was so startling she began to tremble. She moved to a chair and sat down. "How did…when?" She suddenly became incoherent and couldn't form a sentence.

MacPherson leaned down. "Would you like a glass of water, Mrs. Manning?"

"No. I'm fine. Just give me a few more seconds to catch my breath, then I'll change and come with you."

She got up and they followed her into the kitchen.

"Julie, see if these detectives would like some refreshment while I go up and change. I'll only be a minute," she said and hurried up to her room.

Trish felt numb as she stared at Robert Manning. This all seemed surreal. Unbelievable. His mouth was free of its normal smirk. The closed lids of his eyes shrouded the sardonic gleam that usually flashed in their depths. Death had vanquished them all. Funny, he looked so at peace. As if he would waken soon. Trish nodded to the medical examiner and he pulled the sheet over Robert's face again.

She turned her head and glanced at the two detectives who were standing nearby watching her intently. What were they expecting? That she would break out in tears? Weep hysterically? She was too numb to do either—even if she had felt the need to weep.

The whole thing was ironic. After two years of wanting this man out of her life, an unknown assailant had ended Robert's life less than a week after she had finally accomplished that goal.

Ironic. Surreal. Unbelievable.

She turned and walked away.

Another place without an elevator!

Wally paused at the foot of the staircase and eyed the stairway like a condemned man about to mount the steps of the gallows. With the exception of riding from one spot to another, he and Brady had been on their feet since the call came in at four that morning. And the extra forty pounds he was carrying around sure weren't doing his feet any good. His dogs were hot and aching, and his stomach was doing the growling for them. Now it was past seven o'clock, he'd missed another home-cooked supper and Betty was sure to chew his ass off when he got home.

Wally reached for the railing and started to climb slowly up the stairs. At least this time it was only one flight. He and Brady were getting too old for the job. Six more weeks 'til retirement, and then no more doughnuts, eating on the run—and no more stairs. Just lazing, fishing and home-cooked meals. He and Betty might even get in some of that traveling they'd talked about doing for the past thirty years.

The man who opened the door to his knock had a tall, well-proportioned body. That was the first thing he checked out now on men. With a quick glance, Wally could see the flesh under the knit shirt was solid muscle. He could only hope this Cassidy wouldn't give them a hard time and they'd end up having to wrestle the guy into cuffs.

How in hell does a guy keep himself in that condition anyway? he thought enviously. Come retirement, he was going to start working out and get back into shape.

Wally flashed his badge. "David Cassidy?"

"Yes."

"I'm Detective MacPherson and this is Detective Brady. We have some questions to ask you, sir. May we come in?"

Cassidy stepped aside and closed the door when they entered. "So, what can I do for you, detectives?"

Wally prided himself on first impressions. After thirty years on the force he could tell guilt or innocence by people's reaction to his mere presence. A twitch, blink or tone of voice usually gave a guy away. This guy seemed on the square.

"Mr. Cassidy, are you acquainted with a Patricia Manning?"

Cassidy's instant look of distress was more of an answer than his words.

"Did something happen to her?"

"According to a witness, Mrs. Manning was seen leaving your apartment about seven o'clock last night. Is that true?"

"What is this all about?" Cassidy asked.

"Just answer the question."

"Yes, that's true. Now how about you answering my question? What is this all about?"

"It's about a murder."

The look of alarm appeared in Cassidy's eyes again. "Murder? Trish was murdered?"

"Trish?"

"Patricia Manning," Cassidy said.

"No, Mrs. Manning is alive and healthy. It's Mr. Manning who's the victim. His body was found in an alley this morning. His throat had been cut."

"Manning!" Cassidy walked over to a chair and sat down. He appeared to be genuinely shocked. Either the guy had nothing to do with the killing, or he was a damn good actor.

"Hard to believe you hadn't heard about it."

The man was lost in thought. He snapped back to attention. "I'm sorry. What did you say?"

"I'm surprised you didn't know." Wally said. "It's been on the tube and radio all day." He walked over and turned on the TV. "'Pears like your TV's working just fine." He snapped it off.

"I haven't played the radio or TV," Cassidy said.

"What about newspapers? The talk's all over town."

"I've been in Virginia on business all day. I just got home when you guys showed up. Of course, you know that already. I saw you two sitting in your car when I came in."

"You a cop?" Wally asked.

"No, but that Crown Vic you were parked in was a dead giveaway. I've seen a lot of you guys in the business I'm in."

"And what kind of business would that be?"

"That definitely is *none* of your business," Cassidy said.

"Mr. Cassidy, did you leave here after seven o'clock last night?" Wally asked.

"No, once I came home, I stayed in the rest of the evening."

"Can anyone confirm that?"

With a derisive snort, Cassidy said, "Perhaps the same person who saw Mrs. Manning leave here."

"So you're not denying she was here?"

"No. She was here for about fifteen minutes."

"What is your relationship with Mrs. Manning?"

"I think I know where this is going, Detective. Am I or Mrs. Manning a suspect?"

"Statistically speaking, Mr. Cassidy, the wife or her lover are always good prospects."

"And what makes you think I'm her lover?"

"A hot-looking broad like her, handsome stud like you. It wouldn't be the first time. How long have you known her?"

"Seven years. We were once engaged, had an argument and I left town. Didn't see or talk to her again until a couple of days ago when we met by accident."

"And you 'got that old feeling,'" Brady said. He smirked at Cassidy. "Right, pal?"

"So you can speak, Detective Brady. I'd begun to doubt it. But you're wrong, pal. We didn't part as friends last night any more than we did six years ago."

"You saying the two of you quarreled last night?" Wally said. "What about?"

"I didn't say we quarreled. And what we talked about is our business."

"Not anymore. It became ours when her husband ended up in an alley with his throat cut."

"You mind if we look around your place?"

"Yeah. It's not for rent."

"We can always come back later with a warrant, smart ass," Brady said.

"You need grounds to get a warrant, officer."

It was clear to Wally that they'd gotten all they were going to get out of Cassidy. He'd cooperated until now, but the guy had just put on the gloves and wasn't going to take any more shoving.

"Let's go," Wally said. "We'll continue this discussion at the station."

"Am I under arrest?"

"Not at this time. We'd like to get a complete statement from you, though."

When Cassidy walked over and picked up the phone, Wally quickly added, "We don't have time for this. Tell your lawyer to meet you at the precinct."

"I'm not calling my lawyer. Ask the operator for Secretary General Jeff Baker or Deputy Secretary Mike Bishop. Preferably Bishop." He dialed a number and then handed Wally the telephone.

After several minutes of talking to Mike Bishop, Wally hung up.

"All right, Mr. Cassidy. We won't take you in. But we want you to come into the station and sign a statement within the next twenty-four hours. I don't care what agency you're with. Let's go, Joe."

"What the hell was that all about?" Joe asked when they returned to the car.

"Cassidy's a fed. Works for the CIA. Manning was under suspicion with them."

"More reason to think Cassidy whacked him," Joe said. "Especially if he's got the hots for the guy's wife."

"I think he was up-front with us. Seems like a pretty decent guy. Not the kind who would commit murder."

"What are you talking about? Those CIA guys are always knocking off people."

"He's in some special ops squad. They go in and rescue hostages and situations like that. Naw, my guess is that he's not the one who killed Manning."

"Then that makes the wife the prime suspect. She's one cold cookie. You notice the woman didn't shed a tear when she identified her husband's body. And she had no alibi for what she was doing last night either. Then we find out from the lady across the hall that the not-so-grieving widow had been with him."

"I know, but my gut feeling is that the wife was telling us the truth, too."

"My money's on the wife. Remember that movie with Barbara Stanwyck where she talked Fred MacMurray into bumping off her husband for the insurance money?"

"Double Indemnity."

"Yeah, that's it. Same thing. She's probably carrying a policy on him big enough to pay off the national debt. She's too hot-looking for him to be cheating on her, and that body is too good a playground to mess up with a fist. So it's definitely her. She probably did it for money. And you know as well as I do that most murders are committed by someone who knows the victim."

"That's true, but you still need to keep an open mind, Joe."

"Open mind? If you figure that broad ain't guilty, I think you kept yours open too long and your brains fell out. And I bet you a bag of doughnuts the boyfriend's in on it, too. With Cassidy's size and build it would be a cakewalk for him to take out Manning. He's even trained to do that kind of thing."

"That doesn't mean he did it. I figure the two logical suspects had nothing to do with the killing. But they're both lying about one thing."

"That he's not banging her," Joe said.

"No, I don't think he is." Then with a wry grin added, "At least for now. But I think they both lied when they implied they don't love each other."

Joe shook his head and merged onto the Beltway. "Geez, Wally, I can't believe it. Thirty years on the force and you still keep hoping for happy endings. Now I know what to get you for Christmas, partner—a book of fairy tales."

Wally chuckled. "Nothing's wrong with 'they lived happily ever after.'"

"Yeah, right. On the insurance money."

Chapter 6

Arms folded across her chest, Trish prowled her room like a caged animal. Thank God her father and Julie were there to ensure her the privacy she needed.

From the time she'd returned home from identifying Robert's body, the telephone had rung incessantly and there'd been a steady stream of the media at the door.

Some of the photographers were even as bold as to prowl around the outside of the house hoping to snap a picture of Manning's widow. Many in the press corps were well aware of Robert's past peccadilloes, and no doubt a number of juicy tidbits would be added to the evening news.

Trish had always been a darling of the press. Her volunteer work and the many charity fund-raisers she had chaired had always been covered with glowing references or pictures of her. And out of respect to her, they had kept the marital problems between her and Robert out of print.

But now they smelled blood and were swarming like sharks in a feeding frenzy.

Trish glanced at the television set. A blond anchor woman was running on ad nauseam about the romance of the victim and his socialite wife, complete with pictures of the bridal couple taken on their wedding day.

"Ghouls!" Trish ranted. "Blood-sucking ghouls!" She snapped off the television and continued to pace.

God forgive her, but she couldn't grieve for Robert. She had grown to loath him, but the Lord knew she had never wished him dead. Only out of her life.

And she couldn't deny she wasn't in love with Robert when she married him—as if she could ever love any man except Dave. But she had entered the marriage vowing to be a good wife to him, only to discover the man she married was a monster.

She stopped her pacing and leaned forward to study her image more closely in the mirror. Faint dark circles formed half moons under her eyes. The circles were not from crying though, they were from her lack of sleep the past few nights. She hadn't shed a tear since Robert's death. Perhaps she had become a shallow heartless bitch? Certainly Dave believed she was.

Trish closed her eyes in anguish and pressed her flushed cheek against the cool, smooth surface of the glass. She'd found out just hours ago that the man she'd married had been murdered, and she still couldn't get Dave off her mind.

She opened her eyes and once again stared at her image. "Robert was an evil man, Trish. There's no guilt in being unable to mourn him. Neither of you were ever husband and wife in mind, heart, or...soul."

With that thought and her conscience finally free of guilt, Trish washed her face and went downstairs to dinner.

The meal was a quiet one. Her father kept stealing sympathetic glances at her until she could no longer ignore them.

"Dad, will you stop looking at me as if you expect me to shatter into pieces any minute."

"I'm just concerned about how you're holding up, baby. I know this is painful for you."

"I'm fine, Dad. I just wish those annoying reporters and photographers would leave us alone"

"They've left for the night. I suspect things will calm down by tomorrow."

"Well, I hope so. I'm sorry to be such a burden to you, Dad. I'm thinking of returning to the apartment now that Robert is—"

"Nonsense. I won't hear of it," Henry said. "You're staying here until this all blows over. What would be gained by isolating yourself in that apartment?"

"There's a lot that has to be done, such as making funeral arrangements, going through Robert's papers and packing up his personal belongings."

"You don't have to bother. I spoke to Chandler Davis."

"Robert's attorney?"

Henry nodded. "Chandler said he'll handle whatever legal transactions are necessary. And I've told my secretary to deal with the funeral arrangements whenever the police release Robert's body."

Trish felt a rush of annoyance. "It wasn't necessary to dump the funeral on Corine, Dad. She has enough to do handling your affairs."

"The arrangements are simple. Robert requested cremation, so there will only have to be a private memorial. Corine does need a list of Robert's relatives though."

"To my knowledge, Robert's only living relative is an uncle who lives in upstate New York."

"Philip Manning?"

She nodded. "I've only met him once, at our wedding, but Robert never had a good word to say about anyone except his uncle Philip. And Ali bin Muzzar, of course."

"Apparently, Robert did think a lot of Philip Manning because he made him his heir."

"Did Robert tell you that?"

"No, Chandler did."

"And how did you know Robert wanted to be cremated?"

"Chandler said it's in his will."

Her annoyance escalated and she put down her fork and tried to get a firm hold on her control. "Frankly, I don't want any of Robert's assets. That's clearly spelled out in the terms of the divorce. But Chandler had no business revealing to you the contents of Robert's will."

"We're old friends, Trish. And he knows I'm involved in your welfare."

"I don't care how much of an old friend he is to you, Chandler Davis should not have revealed the contents of Robert's will to you. Unless you are named in the will. When did you speak to Chandler?"

"He called today."

"I wish you had given me the call. I have a great deal to go over with him."

"I was only trying to make things easier for you at this distressing time, baby. I told Chandler your divorce actions will be dropped at once and are to remain confidential."

"Why would you do that? Carter Powell has probably already filed the divorce papers we signed."

"He hasn't. I spoke to him and told him to delay filing them."

"You had no right to do that."

"Trish, it's just as well the police are not aware you were in the process of a divorce."

"Dad, they know about the divorce. I told them myself."

He frowned in distress. "I wish you hadn't, Trish."

"For heaven's sake, why not?"

"They might think you hated Robert enough to kill him."

"That's ludicrous. Why would I kill him when he was getting out of my life once and for all?"

She was getting stressed out again. Trish took a deep breath and addressed him calmly.

"Dad, I appreciate what you're trying to do. Truly I do. But will you try to understand that I don't need you, your secretary or anyone else taking over my responsibilities. I'm a grown woman and you keep treating me as if I were still a child. When are you going to accept the fact that I'm no longer Daddy's little girl?"

"I think we'd be wiser to postpone this conversation to a later time. You're stressed out right now, baby."

"Yes, I realize that I'm stressed out, but that doesn't mean I'm incapable of functioning as an adult. Dave was right, I don't—"

"Dave? Dave who?"

She wanted to bite her tongue. She never should have let his name slip from her lips.

"It doesn't matter. If you don't mind, I have a headache, and I think I'll go to bed and try to get some rest. This has been an unforgettable day."

"Sit down, Trish," he ordered when she started to get up. Bridled anger now sharpened his tone, and her throat suddenly felt dry.

Trish sank back down and reached for the glass of water at her plate.

"Kindly tell me the full name of the Dave to whom you referred."

This was the very kind of scene she had hoped to avoid. She certainly didn't need this, but it was too late.

To avoid looking at him, she studied the embossed pattern of the damask tablecloth. "Dave Cassidy."

She heard him suck in his breath, and glanced up to meet the displeasure in his eyes.

"So your knight in armor has returned."

"There's no need for sarcasm, Dad."

"When did Cassidy show up?"

"He was the leader of the squad that rescued us in North Africa."

"Oh, my God! Astride a white charger, no doubt."

She tried to lighten the mood. "Actually, it was a gray helicopter."

He wasn't amused. "And you failed to mention this to me."

"What difference does it make, Dad? Dave poses no threat to you. He loathes the sight of me. He made that quite clear when I saw him last night."

"You saw Cassidy last night!"

"Yes, I did." She was coming apart at the seams, unable to disguise her frustration and resentment. "I went to his apartment."

"You went to the apartment of the man you were once engaged to on the very night your husband was murdered. That will read well with the police," her father said with a sneer.

"Get real, Dad. How did I know Robert would be murdered? Furthermore, I was only there for a few minutes."

"Why, Trish? Why would you even go there in the first place?"

"To tell Dave about the diamonds."

She had already said more than she should have, but knowing her father it was too late to back off now.

His eyes narrowed, and he lowered his voice. "What is this about diamonds?"

"Yesterday afternoon I went to the apartment and found a small pouch of diamonds in the safe. I could only assume Robert had put it in there."

"What did you do with it?"

"I left it there, of course. But it didn't make sense to me, so I thought I better tell Dave about it."

"Why in hell would you tell him? Why didn't you come to me?"

"You were gone. And I didn't know what to do, so I went to Dave."

"That was a damn fool thing to do, Trish."

That did it! She tossed her napkin aside and stood up. "You're right, as usual, Dad. I suppose I was just looking for an excuse to see him again. You see, I'm still crazy about him, but he wants nothing to do with me. That should make you very happy. You won, Dad. Break out the champagne. 'To the victor fall the spoils.'" She strode from the room.

Later that evening, driven by the need to stretch her legs, Trish took Ayevol outside for a walk. In the event there was a reporter lurking around, she remained on the grounds of the estate.

As she strolled through the garden, Ayevol scampered ahead of her, stopping to sniff a blade of grass or examine a fallen leaf.

A light breeze ruffled her hair and she raised her face to catch the full measure of the soothing massage. Closing her eyes she took a deep breath and reveled in the sweet fragrance of jasmine and roses that followed in its wake.

"Trish."

Startled by the sudden intrusion, her eyes flew open as a cry of alarm slipped past her lips.

Barking profusely, Ayevol streaked back and sprang at the figure who stepped out of the shadows.

"Hi, boy, how you doing?"

Dave Cassidy knelt down and the excited dog leaped into his arms, attempting to lick his face in greeting. "I missed you, pal."

Trying to avoid the lapping tongue, Dave looked up at her and grinned. "I can't believe he remembers me after all this time."

Trish contained her surprise, but couldn't stop her heart from pounding joyously at this reunion. The three of them were all together again.

Ayevol had been the first gift Dave had given her. Shortly after they'd set up housekeeping together, they'd seen the puppy in the window of a pet store and it'd been instant love between all three of them.

The dog's name was always a source of confusion to people. Many misunderstood and thought it was Eye Full, others Eiffel, but actually, as a secret message to each other, she and Dave had created an anagram for Love Ya when they named the dog.

"Of course he does, Dave. Dogs are like elephants; they never forget."

Trish knew she had to get a better control on herself

before talking further with him. She walked over and sat down in the nearby gazebo that sat in the center of the garden.

For another long moment, Dave and Ayevol renewed their friendship, then Dave stood up and joined her. Traitorous little imp that he'd become, Ayevol stayed at Dave's heels, and settled down at his feet when Dave sat down.

"What are you doing out here, Dave?"

"I was on my way up the driveway when I saw you come outside."

"Why didn't you stop me and come into the house?"

"I prefer talking to you without Henry around."

"He's not home. Would you like to go inside?"

"This will do."

"I imagine you're here because of Robert's murder."

"Are you aware that you and I are suspects in your husband's murder?"

His comment took her by surprise. "No I wasn't. Why would the police suspect you?"

"Because they know you came to my apartment last night."

"But I never even mentioned your name to them."

"Most likely they heard it from Mrs. Graham. She probably saw your picture in the newspaper and called them. The woman means well, but she doesn't realize that some things are better left unsaid."

"I'm sorry, Dave. My going to your apartment last night was a big mistake. Now you're dragged into all this, too."

"It's too late for regrets. I'm in it whether I want to be or not. Has there been any break on the case?"

"Not that I've heard."

"You would have, if there'd been. I can't help think-

ing that pouch of diamonds you mentioned had something to do with your husband's murder."

"I thought it was just a random mugging. The police
said Robert's watch and wallet were taken."

"The killer could have done that to make it look like
a robbery. Did Robert have any enemies?"

"You met him. Do you have to ask?"

"Anyone you know of in particular?"

"Ayevol. He growled every time Robert came near
him." At Dave's impatient look, she said, "Truly, Dave,
I don't know. Robert didn't seem to have many friends.
Ali bin Muzzar appeared to be the closest. I wasn't with
him long enough to meet his friends, and we haven't
done any socializing together in the past year and a
half."

"What about Henry?"

"They seemed to get along well—certainly better
than you and Dad did. Dad always seemed to make excuses to me for Robert."

"Most likely because he knew your husband didn't
pose a threat to him where his little girl was concerned."

There it was again. That same issue that had destroyed
the relationship between them: the tug-of-war over her
between Dave and her father. Would it ever be put to rest?

"We've been there, Dave," she said wearily.

"Did Manning have the diamonds on him when he
was killed?"

"I wouldn't know. I haven't been back to the apartment."

"I think it's important we know."

"Are you suggesting we go there now?"

"I'd like to know."

"Okay, I'll get my keys. Come on, Ayevol." The dog
gave Dave a reluctant look, then trotted after her.

Dave was waiting in front of the garage when she showed up a few minutes later.

"Are you going to follow me?"

"I didn't come in a car."

She looked at him in surprise. "You walked?"

"I had a cab drop me off about a mile from here."

"And you've been prowling around Georgetown in the dark! You know as well as I there are very wealthy and influential people living around here. You're lucky you weren't spotted and shot as a prowler or even a terrorist trying to assassinate one of my congressmen neighbors."

"I'm trained to move around unobserved. The keys, Trish." She dropped the keys into his outstretched palm.

Trish savored their riding together again in the intimacy of a car. It always made her so aware of his masculinity. His long fingers on the wheel, the smell of his aftershave.

She leaned her head against the smooth leather and closed her eyes, recalling that long-ago night when she had met Dave for the first time. He had driven her home from the party.

The memory was still so vivid—so pure.

From the time her father had introduced them Trish had purposely avoided Dave Cassidy. Stolen glances at him didn't count. The man was lethal. Sensuality oozed through every pore in his gorgeous body, and like most of the women in the room—married or single—she couldn't keep her eyes off him. No man had ever attracted her as much as he had, and it scared her. It gave him an advantage over her.

Yet, when he approached her two hours later, she was too intrigued to reject him.

"I'm ready to leave anytime you are."

"As a matter of fact, I was just considering leaving. Is that an offer to drive me home, Mr. Cassidy?"

"The offer's for whatever you wish, Miss Hunter."

If she'd had any sense she would have backed off then, but the attraction between them was too strong, too irresistible.

He was unexpectedly silent as he wove through the Beltway traffic with the same air of confidence as he moved. Some might mistake it for arrogance—Trish recognized it as a man secure with who and what he is. That quality attracted her more than his obvious physical ones—which were overwhelming in themselves.

He pulled up at the front door of her father's house but kept the car idling, which gave her a clue to his intentions to leave.

Turning to her, he grinned. *"So at last I've met Patricia Hunter. Exquisitely beautiful. Brainy. Pleasant. Selfless charitable volunteer—and according to the gossip, the boss's pampered daughter."*

"And I've finally met David Cassidy," she replied. *"Dangerously handsome. Phi Betta Kappa. Summa cum laude. Rising star on the corporate horizon—and according to the gossip, the anointed future head of Hunter International."*

"That won't be for a while, Miss Hunter."

"Does that bother you, Mr. Cassidy?"

"Not in the least. On the contrary, it could be an unexpected company benefit—plenty of time for us to get to know each other."

"I'm not included in the firm's cafeteria plan, Mr. Cassidy."

"I hope not. I'd prefer to keep this just between us."

"Keep what?"

"What's going to happen between us."

"Which is nothing. I don't date men who work for my father."

"Until now."

"Are you always this confident?"

He chuckled. "I try to be, but I admit my ego's taken a hit a time or two."

She couldn't help smiling. "And you can chalk one up again, Cassidy, because you're not about 'to go where no man has gone before.'"

A dark brow arched in amusement. "Does that mean you're a virgin, or a Trekkie?"

"I thought I made myself clear, Mr. Cassidy. I don't date the help."

He sobered, and drew her slowly into his arms. Lowering his head, his voice a husky whisper, sent a shiver down her spine.

"What's going to happen between us is inevitable. And you can't stop it, Trish, any more than I can."

His lips were firm and warm, and her body tingled under the pressure. At first she responded out of curiosity—and then out of need as the kiss deepened. Rising passion sparked her desire like a flame to dry wood, sending an exquisite liquid warmth surging through her, flooding her senses and loins.

And from that first, rapturous kiss, Trish knew she was his forever.

"Where do we go from here?"

His voice snapped her out of her reverie. "I beg your pardon?"

"The address, Trish."

"Don't you remember the way?"

"Why would I?…You mean it's the same apartment we…" He cut off what he was about to say.

"Yes it is." Trish was too wrapped in her own problems to give much notice to his. Nothing like being jolted from an erotic daydream just when she was getting to the good part.

She gave him a disgruntled look and hunched down in the seat.

Six years and the place looked exactly the same to Dave. Maybe a few different names on the mailboxes, but even the carpeting and color of the paint was the same.

As they rode up in the elevator, he thought of how often they'd steal a kiss or fondle each other on the way up to their floor.

The hall's walls and carpeting might have been the same, but when they entered the apartment there was a big change.

Everything in the living room was a contrast in black and white, from black painted patterns on the white walls to low-slung black leather couches and ottomans against white carpeting.

She went over to a shiny ebony end table, and leaned down to press a concealed lever. A panel sprung open, revealing the combination dial of a safe.

"So when did you have a safe installed?" Dave asked as he glanced around.

"Robert had it built right after we were married. He was quite paranoid, actually."

"Judging from the way he died, he might have had good cause to be."

Intrigued, Dave walked over to examine it. The metal safe was entirely boxed within the wooden cabinet built to match the veneer and pattern of several such tables in the room. Unless you were aware of it, one would never suspect a safe was concealed within it.

"Inventive," he said.

"Very! Actually, there was nothing pedestrian about Robert. His theory was, 'everyone looks behind the pictures on the wall for a safe, but would never think that it'd be right next to the couch.'" She began to spin the dial on the safe.

What the hell am I doing here? The question repeated over and over in his head as she worked the combination of the safe's lock. The whole scene was surreal to him, like an out-of-body experience. The art deco furniture and decorations only added to the irrational imagery, but this was still the same building...same apartment that he and Trish had shared.

Her father had harped at them for not investing in a condo or house. They had decided to hold off until after they were married. Considering the breakup that followed, it had been a good decision.

Whatever he looked at conjured up an image of a past memory: a barefoot Trish frying bacon and eggs on a Sunday morning wearing a frilly bib apron with only a pair of black silk panties and bra underneath it.

The two of them cuddled on the couch in the den watching television.

The living-room floor where they'd "christened" the apartment the day they moved in.

He avoided looking toward the bedroom they had once shared. The thought of her in bed with Manning made him break a sweat.

Let it go, Cassidy. It's all in the past. Keep it there where it belongs. You're no longer that same person and neither is she.

Maybe seeing Trish again was a good thing. Perhaps it would make him face the issue once and for all and rid himself of the haunting memories.

"They're gone!" Trish exclaimed.

"Or soon will be, I hope," he replied with determination.

"What?" she asked.

"Nothing," he said quickly.

For God's sake, Cassidy, stay focused.

"The diamonds are gone. There's no sign of the pouch."

"So much for the diamonds. Manning either disposed of them or had them with him when he was murdered. It's the Agency's problem to figure it out. Let's get the hell out of here, Trish."

They had no more pulled out when his cell phone beeped.

"We're holding up the card game waiting for you," Mike Bishop said.

"I'm on my way." Dave hung up. It was the code between them to call in the squad.

"I have to go. You can drop me off at the next corner. I'll flag a cab."

"I can take you home, Dave."

"That's not necessary."

"Okay, if that's what you want," she said.

Trish pulled over and he got out. "If I were you, I'd let Baker and Bishop know about this latest development with the diamonds."

"I will. Thanks for your help, Dave."

As she drove away, a Crown Victoria followed her. He recognized the two detectives, MacPherson and Brady, as it drove past. So the police had tailed them tonight. That meant Trish was still under suspicion.

Well at least with the cops following her, he'd know she'd make it home safely.

I wonder if the call was from a woman?

Trish pondered the thought as she drove away. He'd

certainly jumped to attention when it had come in. She had to put him out of her mind. In the times they'd interacted in the past few days, Dave had made his feelings clear to her. He'd gone on with his life, while she had wallowed in the thought of what might have been.

If only they had had a child together. She would have someone to love and cherish the rest of her life— a living reminder of the only man she could ever love. Now that would never be.

Maybe she shouldn't give up so easily. Maybe she could spark a reminder in him of how great it had been when they'd been together. Perhaps she could somehow convince him she hadn't stooped to the level he thought she had. Every time he looked at her with loathing, it was like a knife thrust.

Yet, he'd called her Trish tonight instead of Mrs. Manning. That was a good sign, wasn't it? Just maybe his guard was starting to slip.

Maybe when all this horrendous nightmare was over, Robert's murder resolved…maybe then they could at least become friends.

She never noticed the car that drove slowly past as she turned into the driveway.

Dave couldn't sleep. He glanced around the plane and saw the rest of the squad was asleep except for Addison. The kid was still green. Give him a couple more missions and he'd learn to grab a few hours of shuteye when he had the chance.

Five hours ago he was with Trish, now here he was on a plane headed for Sri Lanka on a mission to go in and rescue an agent who'd been snatched by a rebel group demanding ransom.

He pulled out a map and turned on a flashlight to read

it. Try as he might, he couldn't get Trish out of his mind. He couldn't keep being with her and keep his hands off her. But he knew for sure that the moment he gave in they'd be back in the same rut—facing the same problem that had torn them apart—Henry Hunter.

Maybe by the time they got back, Manning's murder would be resolved. If the police didn't solve it, the Agency was sure to. And there was no doubt in his mind that Henry Hunter would be involved in the murder somehow. And that would break her heart. But whether Henry was guilty or not, no matter what the outcome it would always be the same catch-22 for him and Trish.

But right now he had to concentrate on the mission. There were lives at stake here, which was of far more importance than the fate of Henry Hunter.

Dave once again returned his attention to the map before him.

Chapter 7

Dave finished his debriefing and was in his car about to leave headquarters when his cell phone rang. It was Mike Bishop calling him back.

"What now?" he grumbled, after hanging up. He was tired. Had not slept in over forty-eight hours, and only sparingly prior to that, due to this situation with Trish.

The mission had been successful, they'd gotten the agent out, but the rescue had turned into a bloody firefight. Rick Williams had taken a round in the arm and Pete Bledsoe had suffered a shoulder wound.

"Sit down, Dave," Mike said. Dave knew the tone. Bishop was pissed. "How're Bledsoe and Williams?"

"Surface wounds. Could have been worse. They'll be laid up for a week or so."

Then he lashed out with what was on his own mind.

"Not more than a dozen rebels! Where in hell did that

come from? The place was swarming with armed guards. We were outgunned about twenty to one and were lucky to get out of there with just two men wounded."

"I'm sorry, Dave. Intel sure blew this one. But that's not why I called you in here. Why didn't you tell me you knew Patricia Manning when I briefed you for the North Africa mission?"

"She was Patricia Hunter when I knew her. I had no idea she was Manning's wife. I'd had no contact with her since we broke up six years ago."

"You've had plenty of time to tell me since then."

"You talked to Detective MacPherson the other day. That's why they were questioning me."

"It would have helped if you'd told me about Manning's wife. The detectives showed up here yesterday and cold-cocked me with that information. You're a suspect in Manning's murder."

"Yeah, I know. I gave them my statement a couple of days ago. I'd hoped they'd have the damn thing solved by now."

"Well, they don't." He stood up. "We're due in Baker's office."

When they entered Dave got a shock that zapped the tiredness right out of him: Trish was seated in one of the chairs.

"Sit down, gentlemen," Baker said. "Good job on the mission, Agent Cassidy."

"Thank you, sir," Dave said, drawing up a chair.

"You know Mrs. Manning, of course," Baker said, casting a discerning glance in Dave's direction.

"Yes, sir."

"Then shall we cut to the chase?" Baker said. "Agent Cassidy, as you know, the Agency is anxious to capture

Colin McDermott. Our theory is that McDermott and Manning were in some kind of an alliance that involved funding the IRA. Your raid obviously interrupted their transaction. We believe McDermott followed Robert Manning to D.C."

"Mrs. Manning has told you about the diamonds," Dave said.

"Yes. McDermott is either after them or sold them to Manning and did not receive payment for them."

"Did Mrs. Manning tell you the diamonds are missing now?"

"Yes, she did."

"Well, then, maybe he's got what he wants."

"We are confident he doesn't. We do, however, believe he is the one who murdered Manning because of it.".

Dave's money was on Henry Hunter, but he wasn't about to introduce that theory.

"We have devised a plan to draw him out," Baker continued. "Mrs. Manning has agreed to help us."

Dave glanced in surprise at Trish. Any plan of Baker's would clearly put her at risk. Her usually expressive face now appeared enigmatic.

He couldn't help wondering what thoughts were going through that head of hers. She always had a quick and intelligent mind. Her conversations often challenged and stimulated him.

"Mrs. Manning," Dave asked, "are you aware you'll be a decoy?"

"Yes, I am," she said.

"May I ask why you would put yourself at risk?"

"I don't know, Dave. Indirectly, I feel involved. I'd like to clear up my own conscience and any suspicion you all might have regarding me."

He felt pity for her. Was she so naive that she couldn't see that her actions might do more than just draw out McDermott? When the whole truth was known, she could be incriminating her own father.

"And we intend to give her all the protection necessary. That's where you and your squad come in, Agent Cassidy," Baker said, turning back to him. "Since Agents Bledsoe and Williams are recuperating, we are assigning the remaining squad to this duty."

"I understand, sir."

"Well, not quite. Suppose you explain it to him, Mr. Bishop."

Mike's culpable glance gave Dave an uneasy feeling. What the hell had they cooked up now?

"Dave, since you and Mrs. Manning were previously engaged, we thought it would be effective, and would perhaps speed up the outcome, to have the two of you appear together publicly. The more visible you are, the sooner it might draw out McDermott if he thinks Mrs. Manning has the diamonds."

"What do you mean by visible, Mike?"

"You know…appear everywhere together. Dinner, theater, et cetera. You could begin tomorrow by attending Manning's funeral."

Dave couldn't believe it. "Are you all out of your minds? Your plans would make us more suspicious than ever in the eyes of the police." He swung his attention to Trish. "Were you aware this is what they had in mind?" She nodded.

Dave shook his head. "Do you know what people will think and say behind your back? My God, Trish, they'll believe you and I have been having an affair all this time."

"My good friends know differently, Dave. I don't care what others might say."

"We can explain it all once the case is solved, Dave," Mike said.

"Hate to play devil's advocate to this ridiculous idea, but what if McDermott didn't kill Manning? What if McDermott got what he came for? And what if the case is never solved?"

Dave turned to Trish. "You see what you're getting yourself into. You're putting your life in danger, jeopardizing your reputation and you could remain under suspicion the rest of your life if your husband's murder isn't solved."

"He's right, Mrs. Manning," Bishop said. "Think carefully, because if you still agree to do it, you cannot reveal these plans to anyone...your father, your best friend or your childhood nanny if you have one. You and Dave will have to appear as two lovers who have resumed a relationship."

"I've thought it over, gentlemen. I know what I'm doing," Trish said.

"Do I have anything to say about this?" Dave declared.

Baker cast Dave a disgruntled frown. "'Yes, sir,' would be appropriate, Agent Cassidy."

Dave threw up his hands in defeat. It was useless to argue. Everyone's mind was already made up.

"Yes, sir."

"Very well, then I think we all understand the situation," Baker said. "Agent Cassidy, will you be kind enough to drive Mrs. Manning to wherever she wishes? The two of you can work out how you intend to proceed." He broke into a crooked grin. "It's a tough assignment, Dave, but the Agency has confidence in your ability to execute it."

Dave was silent as they left the building and headed

to his car. He had to walk off some of his anger before
he tried to say another word. Fortunately she knew him
well enough to remain silent until he did.

"Where to?" he asked as they buckled up.

"You can drop me off at the apartment. I've been
packing up Robert's belongings."

"And what's the schedule for tomorrow?"

"Just a private memorial. His uncle, my father, his
secretary, several of the firm's top brass, Robert's lawyer and a couple of my closest friends will be the only
ones in attendance."

"And a gaggle of uninvited reporters and gawkers."

"I can't do anything about that, so don't blame me."

"Why in hell did you agree to this arrangement?" he
said as he wove through traffic.

"I explained that in Mr. Baker's office. I feel I should
do something."

"Did you tell Baker about our past relationship?"

"I told Mr. Bishop."

"Why?"

"As I told you the other day, Dave, I felt telling the truth
would avoid any further awkward situations between us."

"It sure worked," he scoffed.

"So I've made another mistake. Seems like that's all
I do. One disaster after another. What would I do without all you Monday-morning quarterbacks reminding
me of what I've done wrong?"

He was too tired to argue and was silent the rest of
the way. When they reached the apartment, he got out
and went inside with her.

"Since you're under my protection now, I'll check
out your apartment before I leave. As soon as the squad
gets some sleep, we'll keep a man on you at all times.
Until we do, don't open the door to anyone."

"Dave, there's nothing to worry about. You know this is a secure building."

"There's no such thing as a secure building," he said, and followed her into the elevator.

Several half-filled cartons were scattered in various rooms. Dave checked out the closets and any other place someone could hide. Satisfied, he sat down on the couch while Trish looked up the address of the chapel where Robert's memorial would be held.

"You were busy while I was gone," he said, glancing around at the place. All of Manning's personal articles had all been removed or packed.

"I know. I have a painter coming in next week, and I'm replacing all the furniture."

"Even the safe?" he said.

"Especially the safe. It would be a constant reminder of Robert if I held on to it."

As she paged through the telephone book Trish glanced over at Dave. He had leaned his head back on the couch and closed his eyes. Her heart ached for him.

It had been a rough mission, she could tell by his body language that he was physically exhausted. She quickly wrote down the address and closed the book.

"Here it is."

When he didn't respond, she moved nearer and saw that he had fallen asleep.

Gazing down at him, Trish felt a surge of motherly nurturing. She wanted to tuck him in bed, cover him up and let him sleep peacefully. She suppressed the smile that tugged at her lips.

Right, Trish! If you had Dave in bed again mothering him would be the furthest thought from your mind.

Regardless of what he said now, she would never believe that would be what he'd want her to do either.

Physically, he had a strong sex drive and she knew every spot on that magnificent body of his that could turn him on. Turn her on.

Don't go there, girl.

She quickly turned away and got a pillow and blanket out of the closet, then gently lowered him until he was stretched out. Then she removed his shoes and covered him up.

For a long moment she stood above him, then unable to avoid the temptation, she lowered her head and pressed a light kiss to his forehead.

It was almost midnight and Joe Brady crumpled up the paper cup and tossed it onto the floor of the back seat.

"If I drink any more coffee I'm going to piss in my pants."

"Then lay off it," MacPherson said, swallowing the final draft from the cup he held.

"What'd I tell you?" Brady said. "The guy's gonna spend the night. You convinced now?"

"That don't mean they whacked her husband. We need some evidence."

"Motive, partner. Name of the game is motive. That's as good as evidence. So let's book 'em so's we can get home and catch some shuteye ourselves."

"Motive might impress a jury, but it sure as hell ain't enough to lock them up," Wally said.

"Yeah, but once we start squeezing them, one of 'em will start to squeal. Don't think he'll break, but I figure she'll give him up, and convince a jury with those innocent baby-blues of hers."

"I think you're wrong."

"Okay, so he'll cop a plea and give her up."

"No, I still figure neither of them did it."

"Geez, Wally, get real. The woman's husband ain't even planted yet, and the two of 'em are up there banging away."

"Still doesn't mean they killed him. We've been tailing her for a few days now. I ain't seen one move that's cause for suspicion."

"What do you call tonight? You think they're up there reading bedtime stories to each other? They're guilty as hell."

"They're also too smart to be this careless then. We don't have one bit of evidence on either one of them."

"Look, partner, she says she was just driving around D.C. the night her husband was killed. He says he never went out. We've interviewed a couple of dozen people in the area of the crime scene. Nobody saw a thing. We've interviewed people where Manning worked. No suspect there."

"I'm not so sure. The secretary says she and Manning had an affair, but it ended over a year ago. And his boss came on a little suspicious to me, too."

"Yeah, well he's the wife's father. The old man is probably trying to cover for his daughter. Get real, Wally. The newspapers, Captain Cummings and the D.A. are on our backs. Here we sit doing nothing while the guilty parties are upstairs making up for lost time."

"That's just it. Joe. If they killed him without leaving a clue—keep in mind the M.E. found no trace of either of their DNA on the body—why would they blow it now by sleeping together?" He shook his head. "No, it don't figure. Maybe Manning's got a girlfriend we don't know about. Let's go back to the office and check those credit cards again."

"Credit cards, my foot! Insurance policies, partner. Insurance policies."

Wally turned on the ignition and pulled away.

Chapter 8

The persistent ring of the cell phone woke Dave. He opened his eyes and became aware of sunlight streaming through the windows and sat up in surprise. What in hell was he doing in Trish's apartment? The last thing he remembered was waiting for her to give him an address. Good Lord! He'd fallen asleep and spent the night on the couch.

The ring continued and he dug the phone out of his pocket. "Yeah!" he grumbled.

"Dave, where in hell are you?" Kurt Bolen said.

"Why? What's up?"

"Obviously you aren't. You told us to meet you at your apartment at 0700."

"What time is it now?"

"Eight o'clock. Are you okay?"

"Yeah, I overslept."

He stood up to stretch the stiffness out of his legs and

back. He mustn't have moved a muscle all night. He could hear the shower running, so Trish must have stayed here, too.

"Overslept? Where?"

"On the couch at Manning's apartment. Since we're assigned to guarding Mrs. Manning, I didn't want to leave her alone."

"Apartment? I thought she lived with her father in one of those Georgetown digs."

"Apparently she's moving back in here now that her husband's dead."

"In a situation like this, wouldn't a woman normally move out, not in?"

"How the hell would I know?" Dave grumbled. "Maybe the rent's paid up for the month. Besides, who said this situation was normal?

"You guys get over here fast so I can leave and go back to my apartment to change clothes. I have to attend Manning's funeral at eleven o'clock." He gave Kurt the address and hung up.

He needed a shower to knock the fuzz off his brain. And he was barefoot. Trish must have removed his shoes when she tucked him in for the night. Dammit! This situation could only get worse. He sat down and put on his socks and shoes.

The smell of coffee lured him to the kitchen where a freshly brewed pot was ready and waiting. So Trish had been up and around. He found a cup and sat down on a stool waiting for it to cool enough to swallow.

He was into his second cup when she came out of the bedroom dressed in a white furry robe. Curse him for a fool, but he couldn't help wondering if she had anything on under it. She looked refreshed…and kissable. She always did look good in the morning.

"Good morning." She poured herself a cup of coffee and sat down at the table.

"Why in hell didn't you wake me?" he asked gruffly.

"I thought you needed the sleep."

"That's not your problem. What time did you say we had to be at that service?"

"Eleven o'clock."

"My squad should be here in a few minutes. Then I'll leave to go and change clothes. Do you need a ride home?"

"I have what I need. I've moved some of my things back here."

"Daddy give you permission?"

"You're determined to start an argument, aren't you, Dave? Would you be less grumpy on a full stomach? I'd be glad to make you some breakfast."

"This will do. At least if you had wakened me when you put the coffee on, there'd be less rushing around now."

"Welcome to the twenty-first century, Agent Cassidy. I put the coffee on last night and set the timer for it to go on this morning."

The buzzer prevented him from having to apologize. "I suggest you get dressed while I brief the squad."

She snapped to attention and saluted. "Yes, sir." Then buzzed them in.

"For the sake of propriety, Mrs. Manning, it wouldn't hurt if you made some attempt to appear the grieving widow."

"For whose benefit, Dave?"

"The police department for one. They'll be taking this all in."

"I've been very candid with them regarding my feelings for Robert. I'm not a hypocrite."

"No, but you *are* a suspect…and thanks to you, so am I."

"Anyone who knew Robert Manning is a suspect," she said.

"Good God, lady, he was your husband. You must have one tender memory of him."

"Not one. Robert was not a nice person. The marriage was a nightmare from the beginning."

"Didn't you ever love him?"

"No. And I'm sure the feeling was mutual." She headed for the bedroom.

"Then why in hell did you marry him?" he yelled.

Trish halted and turned to look at him. "Can't you guess? Retribution, Dave. I figured I didn't deserve anyone better."

She continued on to the bedroom and closed the door.

What the hell was that supposed to mean?

Dave remained deep in thought until the knock on the door snapped him back into action.

Before leaving, he gave the men instructions not to let her out of their sight. Then he hurried down to his car. There was a parking ticket on the windshield. The day could only get worse.

Back at his apartment he showered and dressed, then arrived at the chapel just as the service was about to begin.

He glanced around at the small crowd assembled in bored silence staring at a lone pedestal holding the urn that contained the ashes of Robert Manning.

There wasn't a wet eye in sight.

Their attention shifted to him when he came in and sat down next to Trish. A few low murmurs broke the silence.

A somewhat bewildered clergyman offered the usual words of comfort to the mourners then commended Manning's soul to heaven.

Someone in the rear actually snorted.

The whole ceremony didn't take more than fifteen minutes. A black limo immediately whisked Uncle Philip—with the urn of ashes in hand—back to the airport.

Debra and Tom Carpenter, Trish's closest friends, converged on Dave as he waited for Trish to finish speaking to Manning's lawyer.

"Dave, darling, you look marvelous," Deb gushed as they hugged and kissed. "Where have you been these past years?"

"Seeing the world," he said.

Which was more truth than fiction. Trouble was most of what he'd seen had been at night. But he left that unsaid.

Dave had always liked the couple. Beneath Debra's demonstrative facade lay a mind like a steel trap, an inviolable love for the man she married and an inflexible loyalty to Trish. Rumor had it that Henry Hunter had once proposed marriage to her, which neither party would affirm or deny.

She wouldn't be easy to fool. Dave knew Deb would be the real test of whether he and Trish could pull off the appearance of a renewed relationship.

"Please tell us that you and Trish are an item again," Deb said.

"Debra!" Tom reprimanded, shaking Dave's hand. "Sorry, Dave. As you can see, six years hasn't changed my dear wife. I usually just let her out on weekends and holidays."

"Tom, you know you would like to see it as much as I would," she said. "Dave, I hope you didn't get married while you were off seeing the world."

"Now, how could I? You and Trish were the only two I'd ever considered. And you were both married."

"How I love this man, darling," Deb said when Trish came over and joined them. "Let's all go out for an early lunch. I'm dying to talk to him. We've got a lot of catching up to do."

Trish gave him a nervous glance. "I'm sure Dave has business plans."

He slipped an arm around her shoulders. "Nothing I can't get out of, sweetheart. I just have to make a quick phone call." He figured he deserved an Academy Award for his performance.

Dave scanned the spectators. He spied Bolen and Addison across the street and knew Don Fraser had to be around somewhere, too. The two D.C. detectives were also taking in the scene from their blue sedan.

However, there was no sign of Colin McDermott, the one he hoped to see. Not that the elusive terrorist would make himself visible. If he was watching—and Dave's instinct told him he was—McDermott would be disguised.

He stepped away and called Bolen to tell him their intentions. By the time he hung up, Henry Hunter had joined the others. The two men nodded to one another but didn't shake hands.

Two battle-scarred enemies sizing each other up.

Henry made no attempt to hide his displeasure when Trish told him they were all going to lunch. To Dave's relief, her father declined the invitation to join them.

"I see you and Henry are still at swords' points," Deb murmured when Hunter said a quick goodbye and departed.

"Let's not even go there," Dave said quickly.

Trish and Dave agreed to join the Carpenters at a restaurant the two couples had frequented often when they double-dated.

Dave stole a glance at Trish as he wove through traffic. She was quiet and looked despondent. Maybe she was taking her husband's death harder than she wanted people to think.

"You okay, Trish?" he asked.

"Yes, I'm fine. I just don't like deceiving Deb and Tom. I wish we could at least be honest with them."

"I warned you what you were letting yourself in for with this charade. You can still stop it before it goes any further."

"Is that what you would like to do, Dave?"

"It doesn't matter what I would like."

She turned her head and looked at him. "It matters to me."

The slight tremor in her voice drew his gaze. A hint of moisture shimmered on the surface of her incredible sapphire eyes. She looked wounded. Vulnerable. She was hurting.

He wanted to stop the car. Take her in his arms and hold her. Comfort her. Kiss her. He couldn't remember a time he'd ever wanted to kiss her as much as he did at that moment.

He shifted his attention back to the road. He had to stay focused and not confuse sentiment with reality.

Neither of them was the same man or woman they once were.

"Considering how bitter you really feel toward me,

I know it must be difficult for you to go through the motions that you still care."

Once again their gazes met and for an instant his mouth curved with a wistful smile.

"I think it's a double-edged sword for both of us, Trish."

She turned away and gazed out the window.

Once they were seated and settled in, Deb raised her glass of wine in a toast.

"Here's to the four of us back together again."

"Here! Here!" Tom agreed.

"The four of us," Dave said.

He felt as guilty as Trish and wished they didn't have to deceive the couple.

"Well now, Dave, you've got some explaining to do," Deb said. "We haven't heard one word from you in six years. It was as if you'd dropped off the earth. So let's begin with whom you're working for."

"I work for the government."

"Really!" Tom said. "Legislative or executive?"

"I'd rather not say," he said.

"You mean your job is classified?" Deb asked.

"Come on, honey, you heard the man," Tom said. "So stop grilling him."

"I'm just curious." She cocked her head and studied Dave. "I bet you work for the FBI or Central Intelligence Agency. Am I right, Trish?"

"Please keep me out of this conversation," Trish said.

"Now I know I'm right," Deb exclaimed. "Which is it, Dave? Bet it's the CIA."

"Why would you think that?" he asked.

"Because you're tall, dark, handsome—and acting very mysterious."

Dave only grinned.

"That's marvelous! Did you hear that, Tom?" Deb exclaimed. "We can sleep peacefully knowing Dave's running the CIA."

"Debra, I can assure you I am *not* running the CIA," Dave replied with a clear conscience.

Deb broke into a dimpled smile. "It's just a matter of time, darling."

"Deb, do me a favor. For the time being, please don't express your suspicions to anyone."

"Are you working undercover?" she asked.

"That's not the kind of work I do."

She leaned across the table and said *sotto voce,* "Covert operations?"

"You mean as in spy?" he whispered back. She nodded.

He had her, but he could no longer keep a straight face. "'Fraid not, honey. Nothing so *mysterious.* I'm in RATCOM, the Agency's rescue and anti-terrorist unit. We don't infiltrate. We're a special operations force whose primary duty is to rescue hostages."

Good sport that she was, Deb broke into laughter. "You dog! So you were pulling my leg. I guess I deserved it. But why the big secret?"

"We prefer not to advertise. Only our families and close friends usually know."

"And the intelligence departments of our enemies," Tom piped in.

Dave chuckled. "You've got that right, pal."

"I don't think that's funny," Trish said. "You or one of the squad could have been killed the night you rescued me in Morocco."

Deb started to choke on the bite of food she'd just swallowed. "He rescued you in Morocco!" she said breathlessly when she was able to speak.

"He and his squad."

"Girl, we've got to talk."

Deb grabbed Trish's hand and they headed to the powder room.

After lunch they moved to a booth in the barroom and for the next several hours they talked about old times.

And a strange thing happened to Dave. In those same hours he relaxed and forgot about pretense. The woman sitting next to him became the cherished love he adored. Unintentionally, his arm slipped around Trish's shoulders, his hand reached for hers instinctively.

The blinding gleam of a flashbulb jolted him back to the here and now, and the sight of Kurt and Don nudging the photographer away.

The balloon had burst. They said goodbye to the Carpenters and drove to his apartment. Dave shucked the suit and changed into jeans and a knit shirt. Then he packed a change of clothing and some toilet articles.

"Your apartment could use a woman's touch," Trish said when he came out of the bedroom. She picked up a framed photograph of the squad and recognized Mike Bishop among them.

"Was Mr. Bishop a member of the squad?"

"He was the leader."

"I don't see Justin, but I recognize everyone else except this one," she said, pointing to a good-looking, dark-haired man on the photograph.

He came over and glanced at the picture. The essence he emanated encompassed her. Today sitting beside him in the restaurant, feeling his arm around her, the warmth and strength of his hand holding hers, had rekindled the excitement his nearness always generated.

She yearned to feel his arms around her again, the muscular warmth of his body.

"That's Tony Sardino. He was killed in Beirut. Justin is his replacement."

"Oh, I'm sorry."

His grim look warned her not to pursue it any further. She put the picture down and they left and returned to her apartment.

Considering the afternoon they had spent together, alone now in the apartment neither one seemed to know what to say.

"Would you like something to drink?" Trish asked.

"Not right now."

"I had a good time today, Dave," Trish said awkwardly.

"I did, too. It was good seeing Deb and Tom again. They're a great couple."

"Yes, they are."

"The other guys should show up any minute, then whenever you're hungry I'll take you out to dinner."

"Can't we just order in something?"

"The purpose is to draw out McDermott, remember. We have to make ourselves visible."

"Well then, I'll change my clothes while we're waiting." She went into the bedroom and closed the door.

For a long moment he stared at the closed door. This was the damnedest situation he'd ever been in. How much longer could he tell himself he wanted nothing more to do with her, when he ached to hold her in his arms? Something had to give soon. He continued to pace the floor until the others arrived.

"Anyone follow us when we left the bar?" he asked.

"Two guys in a blue Crown Victoria," Justin said. "They looked like fuzz."

"They are. They're the detectives investigating Manning's murder."

"Some guy left the bar right after you and Mrs. Manning did," Don said. "But he took a cab in the opposite direction."

"Anyone among the gawkers at the chapel?"

Kurt shook his head. "Negative. No one stood out. None of us saw anyone who resembled McDermott among them."

"You have to keep in mind it could be someone in his organization. There are plenty of IRA sympathizers in this country."

"Dave, we aren't experts in this field," Don said. "We depend on our instincts more than expertise."

"I know that, but I can almost smell that SOB. He's watching."

"If he is, then he's probably made us, too," Don said.

"Maybe not. I think Trish and I—I mean, Mrs. Manning and I—put on a pretty good performance today."

"I'll say," Justin said. "You sure could have fooled me."

"Well, we'll give it another shot tonight. I'll take her out to eat supper."

"What's the game plan for later, Dave?" Don asked. "Draw straws for who spends the night?"

"I'll spend the night again. It will keep up the impression that she and I have a thing going."

However, the thought of another night on the couch sure as hell didn't appeal to him.

"Okay, you guys cover us while I take her out to eat. Once we get back, you can call it a night, but be back here at 0700."

Trish came out of the bedroom wearing a pair of jeans and a halter top. She had looked classy in the plain black dress she'd worn earlier, but seeing her now, dressed casually, with her long legs and that trim tush of hers encased in tight jeans, she looked flat-out sexy.

And it showed on the faces of every guy in the room—including his own.

"Hi, ma'am," Justin said, when he stopped gaping.

"Gentlemen, since it appears we're stuck with one another for a while, please drop the formality. My name is Trish."

"Whenever you're ready to eat, Trish, we'll go out to dinner, and then come back here. I'm bunking here again tonight."

Her expression never changed, and he couldn't help but wonder what she thought about him spending the night again.

He didn't care whether she liked it or not. After all, none of this whole stupid affair was his idea.

They ate pizza and drank sodas at a fast food restaurant and then went back to her apartment.

Once they were safely settled inside, Kurt Bolen called and signed off for the night.

Neither of them were interested in watching television, but were at a loss of what to talk about—when there was so much to be said.

Trish had changed into her nightgown and the cuddly white robe she had worn that morning. She'd brushed her hair out and it clung to her shoulders like black satin. Try as he might, Dave found it hard to keep his eyes off her as she paged through a magazine.

"How about playing cards or a board game?" he asked finally.

"I don't have either here right now. I haven't moved most of my things over yet."

"What about that word association game we used to play. We always enjoyed that. Pick a word from that magazine you're reading."

Trish flipped open the magazine. "Bittersweet," she said, keying in on the color of a silk blouse.

It was up to him now to come up with another oxymoron relating to the topic of something both bitter and sweet.

"Sweet pickles," he said.

"Sweet and sour salad dressing," she countered.

"Ahh, white chocolate."

"That doesn't fly."

"Why not? That's an oxymoron. It's two opposite colors. Either chocolate or white. "

"That may be so, but both are sweet, so where does the bitter come in? Sorry, Cassidy, you lose."

He thought for a moment, then said, "Okay, how about past memories?"

"What? That's not an oxymoron. Both words refer to something that's taken place in a period before the present."

"Yes, but past memories can be both bitter and sweet."

"You're splitting hairs, Cassidy." She looked at him woefully. "But I guess you're right. At least our past memories are."

"Let's not go there, Trish."

"I don't intend to, but maybe you'll answer a question that's been on my mind since North Africa?"

"What's that?"

"Why are you doing it?"

"Doing what?"

"Risking your life working for the CIA."

"How about truth, justice and the American way?"

"Oh, right!" Trish scoffed. "I'm as patriotic as anyone, but I'm not buying it. For heaven's sake, Dave, you could probably write your own ticket at most Fortune 500 companies. So what's the real reason? Does it have something to do with our breakup?"

He'd never discussed the breakup with anyone, not even Mike Bishop, and they had become close friends since he joined the Agency. He'd carried the truth inside him, eating away like a cancer. Maybe this was as good a time as any to cut it out and start healing.

"When I left, Trish, I made up my mind to get as far away from the life I had as I could. I joined the navy, became a SEAL, and when my enlistment was up, the CIA recruited me. That's it."

"No, it's not, Dave. That's too simplistic. There's got to be a deeper reason.

"Dad always said you have one of the sharpest business minds he's ever encountered. I can understand why you'd want to leave D.C. because of our split, but that doesn't explain why you'd join the military instead of starting a business of your own."

"I admit my enlistment was impulsive. But it seemed like the perfect answer at the time. Once I signed the enlistment papers there could be no changing my mind or turning back."

"I've always thought of you as one who could stay focused once you committed yourself. Did you really feel such an extreme measure was your only option?"

"Trish, from the time I entered college the pressure was on to succeed. Well, I'd had it. I was sick to death of being considered the boy wonder. I'd become a programmed robot that moved in a world where my identity was judged by what I knew, instead of what I was.

"Then I met you, and it seemed as if the inner person I was seemed more important to you. When we broke up, I made up my mind to get as far away from corporate ladders, stock options and fiscal profits as possible. And I didn't want a commission, so I told the navy nothing about my background or qualifications. Do you understand?"

"I understand what you're saying, but it sounds more like a cop-out to me."

"Maybe it was in the beginning. But once in the service I had to take orders instead of give them. The men and women with whom I came in contact accepted the person I was. They didn't require a résumé to make a judgment. I was accepted for myself, not what I could do for them.

"Then when I became a SEAL, I learned the real meaning of teamwork. I worked with men who'd put their lives on the line to save mine, not men who would trample over me to get my job.

"Sure there's a physical risk involved, the money sucks and for damn sure there's no stock options. But when you look around after a mission knowing you all made it through and see the grins on the faces of the guys, it's a damn sight more rewarding than a big bonus check. I could never go back to corporate America."

"Sounds like there's no place for a woman in your life either?"

"Been there. Done that."

She jumped to her feet. He'd struck a chord. For the first time in the past week he saw the flush of hot anger in her blue eyes.

"You self-serving bastard! You've just pushed one button too many. No matter how you feel now, how dare you tarnish the beautiful, tender moments we once shared with that disparaging, cavalier remark."

She stormed into the bedroom, slamming the door behind her.

Dave charged after her like a raging bull and burst into the room. "Where in hell did that come from?"

"Where? I'll tell you where, Agent Cassidy. I've tolerated your bitter attitude, I even told myself I deserved it, the same way I've blamed myself for six years.

"From the moment I opened my eyes on that helicopter, I've walked on eggshells around you, have borne your insinuations that I've sunk to moral degeneration. I even agreed to make myself a decoy as an excuse to be with you. And all because I was so relieved just to see you again, to be able to sit across a table from you, feel the excitement of your nearness the way I once did."

She snorted and threw up her hands in contempt.

"Boy, if they handed out trophies for being a blind, lovestruck fool, I'd have a shelfful. Why, you're nothing more than a self-centered chauvinist, David Cassidy. Everything is about you. Your pain. What *you* went through.

"Well what about my pain? What I was suffering? At least I didn't run away."

"Like hell you didn't. The first thing you could think of was running back to Daddy."

"And I came back to you the next day."

The scalding retort was as much an accusation as it was a rebuttal. It hung on the air like a crushing weight that pressed the fury from her.

"But you were already gone, weren't you, Dave?" she said in a subdued tone. "Did you have your bags packed before I took off your ring?"

"You know better than that. I waited all night for you, but you didn't come home. And I finally realized you weren't going to. So you're right. I ran as far away as I could."

"If only you had called, written, given me one sign, I would have waited for you forever," she said. "I tortured myself with thoughts of you hurt or even dead. I begged Kim to tell me where you were, but she said you swore her to secrecy. I even hired a private detective to try and trace you, but he came up with nothing."

"So you married Robert Manning? Why, Trish? Why him of all people? And don't try to tell me in order to punish yourself."

"No. I knew Robert only married me to secure a safe position with my father. He didn't love me any more than I did him."

"That doesn't explain *your* motive."

She raised her head and looked him right in the eyes. "To have a child. I needed a purpose to go on. So I decided to have a child to love and nurture."

"So why didn't you?"

"When I found out how sick Robert was, I knew it wouldn't be fair to any child to have him for a father."

She raised her head with wounded defiance. "So you see, I lost that hope, too."

She sat down on the bed and kicked off her shoes. "But now I see the light. Tonight I've finally seen the reality that there will never be a you and me again. For the past six years I've let you—wittingly or unwittingly—screw up my life by carrying a romantic belief that one day you'd come back and free me from the wretched hopelessness in which I existed and we'd live happily ever after.

"But in truth, Dave, you're not my knight in shining armor. You're my dragon."

Trish walked over to the dresser, and pulled off her earrings.

"Now, if you don't mind, I'd like you to get the hell out of my room so I can go to bed."

He came over and spun her around to face him. "You had your say, now it's my turn. Who in hell do you think I've been thinking about for the past six years? There hasn't been a day that I haven't thought about you."

"You knew where to find me," she accused.

"Do you have any idea how often I picked up a telephone to call you just to hear your voice? The sound of your laughter? Wondered who you were with? Who was kissing you? Making love to you?"

"Then why did you stay away?"

"Because there's no solution to the problem between us, Trish. It's not all about me. My needs. It's all about the three of us—you, me and Daddy dearest."

"Not again! I'm so sick of the immaturity of that argument. You and my father are obsessed with the issue."

"You've got a convenient memory, lady. Have you forgotten I was all for going to Vegas and getting married? But that would have pissed off the old man, wouldn't it?"

"You accused my father of being dishonest," she flared back. "What did you expect me to do?"

"I believe there's a song about standing by your man. And guess what, baby, that doesn't mean Daddy. It means the man you claim to love. The guy you intended to marry."

"Good lord, you and my father aren't competitors. They're two entirely different kinds of love. You're supposed to be the bright one, Mr. Phi Beta Kappa, so stop making it sound like some kind of reverse Oedipus complex."

"I'll tell you what I do know. When this McDermott mess is finally resolved, your father's going to be involved and your heart will be broken. The first one you'll look to blame will be me, because I'll be mixed up in bringing him down. That's why there's no hope for us again. That's why I ran before. Why I'll have to do it again."

Her eyes glistened with tears. "You don't know for sure he's guilty just because you think he's dishonest."

She was hurting already and it was tearing him apart to witness her heartache.

"Trish, I don't want to hurt you, but it's going to happen."

"You were wrong before. Dad explained the misunderstanding to me. There was no money laundering going on. The Irish company *did* ship ball bearings. They bought them from a supplier. Dad dropped them as clients after that."

"Then what did Manning have on your father to keep you from divorcing him?"

"I assumed it was that same issue you thought you had. It would have been very bad publicity for the firm, even if it wasn't true."

"So he let you become a sacrificial lamb to a rotten pervert in order to save his own ass. But now that the CIA is involved, your father's going to get nailed, Trish. You better prepare yourself for it."

"Did you tell them about Dad?"

"No, I couldn't. For your sake. But McDermott will when we catch him. And we will catch him, Trish."

She looked up into his eyes, her anguish as naked as the errant tears trickling down her cheeks.

"Tell me the truth, Dave. I have to know. Do you hate me for what I've done to you?"

Her misery was like a vise squeezing his heart. He couldn't pretend any longer. The attraction between them was too overpowering, emotions too tenuous to control. The truth was no longer deniable.

"I wish I could hate you, Trish. It would make it so much easier."

He left her staring, stunned.

Chapter 9

Once in the living room, Dave glanced at his watch. It was only midnight. It was going to be a long night. He sat down on the couch and removed his shoes and the gun strapped to his leg, then tucked the weapon under a pillow on the couch.

He had too much on his mind to sleep, so he tried the TV. Surfing the channels, he found nothing to watch except a review of the day's news, reruns of old sitcoms, and a nineteen-thirties Western. He snapped it off and put aside the remote.

He got up and went over to the window. D.C. was asleep. Not even a car moved on the street. He could use a walk, but that would mean leaving Trish alone.

Restless, he went back to the couch and picked up the magazine she'd been reading. He began to page through it until he realized it was a woman's fashion magazine. What in hell was he doing!

Disgusted, he flipped off the lights and lay down. After ten minutes he gave up trying to sleep and padded barefoot into the kitchen to get a drink.

Glass in hand, he leaned back against the counter, stretched out his legs and crossed them, then stood in the dark and dwelled on his argument with Trish.

He should have kept his mouth shut. He'd lost his cool and allowed his emotions to do his thinking. On a mission that kind of carelessness could get them all killed. Here it muddied up an already grimy situation.

Then he heard it: the telltale click of the door lock.

Dave straightened up. Someone had either just entered or departed. He'd bet his reputation that it was the first.

He carefully placed the glass on the sink, and cursed himself for removing his gun earlier. He had no idea which drawer the knives were in, and didn't dare risk taking time to search for one.

Besides, this was his element—darkness his weapon.

A shadow bounced along the living-room wall and Dave moved cautiously to the entrance of the kitchen. His eyes had long adjusted to the darkness and he made out the figure of a man holding something in his right hand.

A quick scan of the room indicated the intruder was alone, so he stole soundlessly across the room. His hand brushed a tabletop and encountered the television remote. On impulse he picked it up, moved closer to the intruder's back, and then pressed the power button on the remote.

Fortunately, the cowboys and Indians were still shooting it up on the tube. Startled, the intruder jerked his head toward the sudden sound of gun blasts and light coming from the television set.

Dave sprung at him, and wrapped an arm around the man's neck in a chokehold.

"Drop it or I'll break your neck."

"Okay," the man cried out.

As a folded newspaper fell to the floor, Dave recognized the intruder. It was the last person he expected it to be. Releasing him with a shove, Dave sent the man stumbling backward onto the couch.

"What are *you* doing here?"

Dave switched on the lights and then walked over and turned off the television.

"I came to talk to Trish," Henry Hunter said.

"Ever hear of the telephone, Henry?"

Henry Hunter glared at him with contempt. "I might ask the same thing about you. You almost killed me." He sat up and adjusted his clothing.

"Too bad. I must have lost my touch." Dave reached under the pillow and pulled out the gun.

At the sight of it, Hunter's eyes looked near to bulging out of the sockets.

"What are you going to do?"

Did the bastard really think he intended to shoot him?

"So what was so important, Henry, that you had to come here at this time of night?"

Hunter pointed to the newspaper he had dropped. "See for yourself."

Dave picked up the folded paper. It was the early edition. On the front page of the style section was a picture of Trish laughing up at him as they sat with his arm around her shoulders.

The caption read: Merry Widow Mourns Murdered Mate. He scanned the accompanying article:

Following the memorial service for her murdered husband, Robert Manning, socialite Patricia Hunter Manning spent the afternoon in the company of an old friend. Sources indicate it's her former fiancé, David Cassidy. The two appeared to be very chummy; could be instead of a funeral dirge our Trish might be humming "Seems Like Old Times."

The article went on to touch on the grisly details of the murder and say that the killer had not been apprehended. It then closed with a reference to Hunter's position in the community.

It was the very thing the Agency hoped would draw out McDermott. However, Hunter was not pleased at all.

"I might have known your showing up again would cause problems. Are you satisfied that you succeeded in getting even *my* name smeared in the gossip section of the paper?"

"Be patient, Henry. As soon as you're nailed for Manning's murder, it'll be the front page."

"Manning's murder? What the hell are you talking about?"

"My money's on you, Henry."

"I swear to you, I didn't murder Robert Manning."

"Give Trish a break and don't make the same oath to her. You've lied to her enough. And I'm not buying your reason for coming here after midnight was to show her a damn picture in a gossip column."

Henry slumped back and lowered his head. He looked vanquished. Was there actually a crack in his armor?

"Is Trish okay?" Henry asked.

"What do you mean? As far as I know she is."

"I mean, did anything occur out of the ordinary to-night?"

Damn straight! He had walked out of that bedroom when all he could think of was making love to her. "Where is this going, Henry?"

Hunter glanced up at him and fear glittered in his eyes. "Trish tells me you were on the squad that got her and Robert out of Morocco."

Dave neither confirmed nor denied it, but waited in silence for Henry to continue.

"I want your word that you won't repeat to anyone what I'm about to tell you."

"I don't buy a pig in a poke, Henry, so I'd never make a promise like that."

"Even if it affects Trish?"

"Little late for your concern for her, isn't it, Daddy? I covered your ass once for her sake, so you've used up your get-out-of-jail-free card."

"Damn you, Dave, this is serious. Trish is in danger."

"What kind of danger?"

"If you repeat this to anyone I'll deny it," Henry said. "Colin McDermott called me tonight." He glanced up to see if he had Dave's full attention.

He had it all right.

"Who's Colin McDermott?" Dave asked.

Hunter snorted. "Let's not play games. McDermott asked me if I got the calling card he left for me," Henry continued. "At first I didn't know what he meant, until he said that if I didn't give him back the diamonds and five million dollars, Trish would meet the same fate."

"You're saying McDermott admitted killing Manning."

"What does it sound like to you?" Hunter snapped.

"Sounds like you could be trying to convince me that you didn't kill him."

"I didn't kill him! Dammit, Dave, don't you understand? I don't have any diamonds and McDermott's threatened to kill Trish."

"That's so not going to happen," Dave said.

"He's not bluffing. He means what he said. The man's a cold-blooded killer."

"Like I don't know that. I figured you were dealing with this terrorist, Henry, and Manning was your leg man. Is that why you encouraged Trish to marry him?"

"That's not the issue right now. Keeping Trish safe is."

"I'm not going to let anything happen to her. In the meantime, haul your ass into the CIA and tell them what you've just told me. Maybe if you cooperate with them, you won't have to do time."

"I'm not going to prison, Dave. I'll make you an offer. You take Trish some place where she'll be safe. Money's no object. I'll handle McDermott."

"What makes you think he won't kill you instead?"

"He's a smart man. He's not going to cut off the money source. With both Robert and bin Muzzar dead, I'm the only one he's got to turn to."

"Knowing what you do about him, you'd continue to do business with him? For God's sake, why would you risk your life and Trish's for a damn bag of diamonds! You don't need the money."

"There's no such thing as too much money. But I don't do it for the money. I do it for the excitement of getting away with it."

"Excitement! The man's responsible for the death of innocent people. You're playing a game with people's lives. You're even sicker than I thought."

"I don't expect you to understand. Everything has to be by the book with you," he scoffed. "Mr. Straight-and-Narrow Cassidy. All brains and no guts. Did you think I'd let my daughter waste her life married to a prick like you?"

"What's going on here?"

Both men spun in surprise to see Trish standing in the doorway of the bedroom.

"Will the two of you please lower your voices before you wake the whole building with your shouting. Dad, what are you doing here at this time of night?"

"Delivering the newspaper," Dave said. He went into the den to get away and closed the door.

Confused, Trish turned to her father. "What happened? What are you and Dave quarreling about now?"

Henry tossed her the newspaper. "See for yourself. The minute he shows up, you make a fool of yourself."

Trish read the article and then put the paper aside. "It's just some spiteful reporter earning his pay. Deb and Tom were sitting in the same booth with us and we were talking about old times."

"And you still had some old times to talk over? Is that why Cassidy's spending the night?" Henry snarled.

"Dad, I love you very much and I don't wish to hurt you, but whom I spend the night with is my business. I've made it clear to you how I feel about Dave, and nothing you say will change that. I made the mistake of losing him once. I won't do it again."

"Don't you have any pride, Trish? Can't you see you're throwing yourself at him? Groveling at his feet for the sake of his vulgar pawing?"

"Dad, please give it up. I'm not going to argue with you over whom I sleep with. But you can be sure it will be Dave if he wants me."

"Mark my words, you'll regret it one day."

"You don't have to tell me about regrets. I've lived with them for the past six years."

In leaving, Henry threw the apartment-door key she'd given him on the table. "Don't say I didn't warn you when it happens."

Trish went into the kitchen and poured herself a glass of orange juice. As she sipped it slowly, she thought of the exchange with her father. He was angry because he hadn't gotten his way, but he'd get over it.

She'd made a choice between him and Dave once, and she wasn't going to make that same mistake again. No matter how much she loved her father and didn't want to hurt him, the woman in her needed more than a pat of approval on the head from her daddy.

She'd done a lot of growing up in the past six years, and she doubted either of the two men realized or recognized it. She'd gone into business, and tonight she'd made another life-altering decision.

Despite what she had said to David during their argument, the instant that door closed behind him she knew she could never give up on him.

She'd misled him—and herself—into believing she could. She was going to fight to hold on to him. Once more fate had brought them together—and she had no intention of defying the gods again.

She was intelligent enough to recognize that maybe things could never return to what they'd been before their split, but she was willing to settle for whatever he was willing to give.

There was nothing standing in the way of them being lovers. And, God forbid, if the day ever came he wanted out of that arrangement, she would have to let him go. Until then, she'd have as much of him as he—and the damn CIA—would let her have.

Somehow she would have to make that clear to him and her father. But from this moment on, she was taking charge of her life. The city's charities would just have to find a different organizer, her dad would have to hire himself a hostess to run his social activities.

Tonight she had discovered a truth she had dared not hoped to believe. Dave had given himself away when he admitted he couldn't hate her. Despite all his actions to the contrary, he still wanted her. And that's all she needed to know. If she couldn't have his love, she was willing to settle for just sex. At least, they'd be together.

So, whether he realized it or not, that control he exercised was starting to crumble. The Walls of Jericho were about to come crashing down. At thirty years of age she was being given a second chance at happiness—another grab at the golden ring on the merry-go-round.

And this time she wasn't going to blow it.

"I'm sorry, Trish."

He moved like a cat. She took a deep breath and turned around. "It's not your fault, Dave. How about a glass of orange juice?"

He grinned. "For breakfast, yes. Right now, a cold beer would taste good."

Lord, how she loved that infectious grin of his; Lord, how she had missed seeing it.

"Sorry, I hadn't planned on you spending the night or I would have gotten some in."

"It's not critical, Trish."

An awkward silence developed between them again, so she turned away and rinsed out the glass, then popped it into the dishwasher.

"Dave, I'm sorry about the argument."

"Don't sweat it. Your father and I will never get along."

She turned around to face him. "I meant our argument. I said some pretty nasty things to you. I didn't mean them."

"We both did. Forget it."

"Did you mean it when you said you've never stopped thinking of me?"

"Dammit, Trish! What do you want from me?" He walked away.

The cowering Trish might have hesitated to pursue the discussion, but the new Trish was on a mission and not to be put off. It was time for Gabriel to blow his horn.

"All I want is the truth, Dave."

He sighed in resignation. "Why can't you let it go, Trish? Words can't change realities. And the reality is that there's no hope for us. You're beating a dead horse." He walked away and went back into the den.

She had some hard thinking to do. There were a lot of issues to be resolved, and she'd probably be better off thinking them all through carefully before blundering blindly into trying to solve them.

Trish returned to her bedroom and closed the door.

The following morning Trish awoke, yawned and with a contented smile raised her arms above her head and stretched.

Trish was very pleased with herself. She had carefully considered all the pros and cons of the changes she intended to make in her life and there was no time like the present to begin to execute them. She reached for the telephone and called Deb. They agreed to meet for lunch.

Practically purring with pleasure, she hopped out of bed and took a shower, then intentionally put on the jogging suit Dave had bought her in Germany and opened the bedroom door.

Dave was in the kitchen. Waking up in the morning

to find Dave in the kitchen was definitely one of the pros in her decision making. Waking up to find him in her bed was a future incentive—the *near* future.

"Good morning. Hmm, that coffee smells good."

"Morning." He poured her a cup and handed it to her.

"So, what's up, Doc?" she said brightly.

He looked at her surprised. "Who told you?"

"Told me what?"

Suddenly, she was struck by what he meant. "Oh, no! Those stupid dwarf names again. Don't tell me you have one, too."

"You always did have a quick mind," he said.

"Heigh ho, heigh ho."

He failed at trying to hold back a chuckle. "And a big mouth."

"And no one knows better than you what I can do with it."

"Now you're hitting below the belt, Trish."

"Your point being?"

"My point is you're not Snow White. So if you think you can turn me on with that kind of gutter talk, Miss Potty Mouth, you're wasting your time."

"So wash out my mouth. Now what's with all this dwarf business, Doc?"

"If you'll drop the Doc bit, I'll tell you."

"Okay, I promise."

"We're known as the Dwarf Squad, and those are our code names with the Agency."

"And which came first—the squad name or the dwarfs?"

"I guess it was the squad name. Remember the picture of the team. Tony Sardino—"

"The one who was killed in Beirut," she said.

Dave nodded. "When the squad was first formed,

Tony was a bashful kind of guy and Mike always called him that. It gave us the idea for the Dwarf Squad and that's how we got our code names.

"If I didn't trust you, Trish, I wouldn't have told you this much. And do yourself a favor and forget that I did. Our code names should be kept confidential."

He said he trusted her. She was breaking through that wall of disdain he'd placed between them.

"Thank you," she said solemnly.

"For what?"

"For trusting me."

"Why shouldn't I? You trust me, don't you?"

"With my life, Dave."

She could feel the treacherous slide of her newly acquired independence. This was no time to weaken. The stakes were too high.

"So what's on your agenda today?" he asked.

"Lunch with Deb. I'm considering investing some more capital into the business."

His arched brows made his surprise apparent. "Really. You and Deb are in business together?"

"Yes. Interior decorators. We have been for the past two years."

"Good for you, Trish. I remember how the two of you always talked about doing that. Glad to hear you finally did start a business."

"Devoting my time to charities was fine, but a couple of years ago I decided I needed something that would give me a chance to be creative. I still volunteer to help whenever I can, but I gave up organizing and running charity events."

"And you're sure that's creative enough for you?"

"My preference would be having a baby. Now that would be creative."

"Why not adopt? I'm sure your father would have a way to cut through the red tape."

"Who knows? I might have to. My biological clock is ticking away. But at the risk of sounding old-fashioned, Dave, I prefer my baby to have a father if at all possible. It's sad enough that single mothers have to raise their children alone due to tragedies or unanticipated circumstances, but, if possible, at least I'd like to start out by giving my baby the best start a child can have—both a loving mother *and* father."

"Sounds like you've given it a lot of thought."

"Definitely. It's not just a passing fancy on my part."

Not in the least, David Cassidy. I've thought about it for a long time. Over six years to be exact.

She cast a yearning glance at him. Haven't you guessed by now, it's always been your child I want to bear.

"Why didn't we ever have a love child, Dave?"

"What brought that on?"

"I don't know. I guess because we're on the subject of babies."

"Frankly, it never crossed my mind when we were together. I doubt it did yours either. Maybe we both are old-fashioned, Trish, and all the pieces weren't in place yet. Isn't there an old saying about love, marriage and *then* a baby carriage. But, in hindsight, considering our bust up, it's just as well that we didn't have one."

"I suppose you're right, of course. You usually are. But you're wrong about one thing, Dave. It *did* cross my mind when we were together."

She stood up and forced a game smile. "I'm going to go jogging."

"Haven't you noticed, it's raining."

"It's just a drizzle. I'll jog in the mall. If you remember, we often did that."

She was out the door before he could even get his shoes on, and he caught up with her at the elevator.

"Why is this a must, Trish?"

"I'm restless, that's all."

"What's wrong with working it out on the treadmill in the weight room?"

"Because I want to run, Dave. It's not necessary for you to come along. After all, we did make the paper. I don't think we have to continually appear in public together."

He didn't want to tell her of her father's warning last night. If Henry was telling the truth, it no longer was a matter of using Trish as a decoy to draw out McDermott—now the trouble would be to keep the bastard from killing her. Maybe the time had come to tell her of her father's warning.

"Hold up a minute," he said when they reached the mall. Her unexpected insistence on going jogging had caused the squad to scramble and he wanted to make sure they were in place.

Raising his wrist to his mouth, he said, "Report." The watches they were all wearing contained transmitters. Instantly the men responded.

"Sneezy clear," Bolen said.

"Dopey clear," Fraser reported.

"Bashful clear," Addison replied.

At least they were all in the strategic places he had assigned to them. He wished Bledsoe and Williams were available though. The mall was big, with plenty of places for a killer to conceal himself.

Thank God the layout of the place hadn't changed drastically in the past years, so as they jogged he was able to analyze the exits and vacant stores as well as getting a good read on the people who were walking the mall.

He concentrated on the men who were McDermott's height. Trouble was, he had no way of knowing who he was looking for if McDermott had an accomplice. It would be a hell of a lot easier if Intel could give them a better description.

The complete circuit of the mall was a mile, and they were on their third time around when Trish began to slow up. He wasn't even winded.

"Have you had enough running for now?" he said.

"How much farther to the entrance?" she asked breathlessly.

"About a quarter of a mile."

"Damn you, Dave, you haven't even broken a sweat."

"You want to finish it in a walk?"

"Of course not. I always do three miles. Trouble is I have to go to the ladies' room."

"There's one coming up." He stopped running and shifted into a fast walk. "So slow down so you don't pull a muscle."

When they reached the rest room, Dave waited outside the door while Trish went inside. A couple approached and the woman went into the ladies' room while the man continued on. Dave felt uneasy.

Within seconds what sounded like a gunshot rang out ahead and he heard some screaming and shouting. His duty was to protect Trish, so he followed his instinct, drew his weapon and entered the ladies' room.

Trish was at a sink washing her hands and the woman had just come out of a stall with a drawn knife.

"Drop it," he yelled.

The woman lunged at Trish, and he fired. His shot caught her in the right shoulder and she fell back as the knife dropped to the ground.

Mouth agape, Trish stared in shock. A black wig

was askew on the head of the fallen figure and the hair underneath was blond.

Dave walked over and kicked the knife well out of the woman's reach, then he checked her pulse. She was still alive. He pulled out his cell phone and called the police. "Are you okay?" he asked Trish, when he finished.

Trish managed to nod. At that moment, Fraser's voice interrupted them.

"I'm at the north end of the mall in pursuit of some guy who fired a shot."

"I see you," Addison said. "I'm on my way."

"We're in the ladies' room near the flower shop," Dave answered. "I just took out a woman who tried to kill Trish." He gave them a quick description of the man who'd been with the woman.

"Sounds like the guy I'm after," Fraser said.

"I'm getting Trish out of here. Sneezy, where are you?"

"Almost right on top of you," Bolen replied.

"Then come here and don't let anyone enter that ladies' room until the police arrive."

"Let's go," he said to Trish.

"What about her?"

"Kurt will handle her." He grabbed Trish's hand and they ran out of the lounge just as Kurt arrived on the scene.

Dave headed back in the direction they came from to a vacant store he'd noticed in passing. He kicked open the door and then raced toward the exit on the opposite end of the store that opened onto the parking lot.

They ran outside into pouring rain—and two security guards with drawn weapons.

"Hold it, you two, and get your arms up," one said.

"I'm a federal agent, officer," Dave said. "My shield's in my wallet."

"Keep those arms above your head," the guard ordered, while the other one pulled out Dave's wallet.

"Okay, you can lower your arms," he said, after a glance at the shield. "What's going on in there? We got a call that a shot was fired."

"You'll find another federal agent stationed at the entrance to the ladies' room near the flower shop on the south end of the mall," Dave told him. "There's a wounded woman in the ladies' room who tried to kill this woman."

"What's your name, lady?" the guard asked.

"It's classified. She's under federal protection right now. There are also two more federal agents inside in pursuit of at least one accomplice we're aware of. Could be more. Will you guys relieve the agent at the entrance to the ladies' room? No one is to enter until the police arrive."

"Yes, sir," one of the guards said. The two men hurried away.

"Why don't we go back and wait for the police?" Trish asked.

"I want you someplace where I know you'll be safe. And maybe we can keep your name out of the papers, too."

"I don't understand all this. Who was that woman? Why would she try to kill me? Is this all to do with McDermott?"

"Calm down, Trish, you're babbling," he warned.

She had begun to tremble and Dave didn't know if it was from fright or the rain. Regardless, he had to get her home.

"Trish, we'll talk about it when I get you back to the apartment. Are you up to some more running?"

"Anything to get out of this rain and get some answers." She took off on a run.

She had spunk. Within the past week she'd been almost raped in Morocco, escaped under fire, shot at in Germany, her husband had been murdered, and now, she had just witnessed the shooting of a woman who had tried to cut her throat.

He had to give credit where credit was due. Trish might have been spoiled and pampered her whole life, but she sure as hell had grit.

Chapter 10

By the time they reached the apartment, both of them were dripping wet. Trish went into her bedroom and Dave headed for the utility room. He stripped down to his shorts and tossed the rest of his wet clothing into the dryer. What the heck, Trish had seen him in briefs before.

After getting a pot of coffee brewing, he called Bolen. The police had arrived on the scene and taken over. They were all at the police station. The fellow they'd been chasing had gotten away. The woman Dave had shot was still alive and had been taken to the hospital.

After hanging up, Dave dialed the Agency. Mike Bishop was not too thrilled. Bolen had already broken the news to him.

"I told Bolen as soon as the police get their statements to go home and dry out. We'll send a couple of intelligence agents to the hospital to talk to the woman when they let us. McDermott's still on the loose so you'd better stay with Mrs. Manning. Apparently she's his next target."

"What about the police? I'm sure they want to talk to me," Dave said, "since I'm the one who shot the woman. Unless she was recognized, I kept Trish's name out of it."

"We're going to need velvet gloves on this one," Mike said. "I'll talk to them and tell them you'll be in to give them a statement. They know from the team's statements they took that Mrs. Manning was an intended victim. Where are you now?"

"At Trish's apartment. We both got soaking wet getting back here."

"Good. Stay put until you hear from me."

Stay put. What choice did he have?—at least until his pants dried.

"What if the cops show up here again and pull us in?"

"Call me."

"That's comforting. Wouldn't the FBI be more efficient at this type of witness protection detail than we are? I'm no expert at this, Mike. A few seconds more and Trish would have ended up on the floor with her throat cut."

Bishop chuckled. "She didn't, though, did she? You did your job." His tone sobered. "Look, Dave, I know how you feel. I went through the same thing when we were protecting Ann. I know it's tough to stay objective when there's an emotional involvement."

"Trish and I are ancient history. But that doesn't mean I want anything to happen to her. I just believe there are agents who are specifically trained for this kind of duty."

"Right. But between you and me, would you trust any one of them to protect her more than you do yourself?"

"Your point being?"

"Ancient history like hell! I caught that picture of you and her in the paper the other day."

"Didn't you imply you wanted us to look like a twosome?"

"You sure convinced me, pal. It's good to see you're happy in your work."

After shedding her wet clothes, Trish stepped into the shower. Soon the steam and hot water routed the chill that had held her in its shivery grasp.

Only then could she think about her harrowing experience earlier that day.

She would be dead now if Mike hadn't interceded. Why did McDermott—if it was McDermott—want to kill her? Surely the man had to know she knew nothing about Robert's illegal dealings.

Until today, she hadn't been frightened. But now she had to wonder when the next attempt would be made on her life.

She finally got out of the shower, wrapped a towel around her head and dried off. Then after putting on a bra and panties, she reached for her white robe.

Desolately, she sat down on the side of the bed. Life was becoming more and more complicated.

That very morning she had made up her mind to turn her life around, and within hours she'd been drawn back into the turbulence of her past with Robert Manning.

The only good thing that had come out of it was Dave's return. Despite her gloom, a smile tugged at the corners of her lips.

Someone's trying to kill me—but you're back in my life. Another bittersweet analogy, isn't it, Dave?

She combed out her hair, gathered up her wet clothing and towels and left the bedroom.

Trish drew up sharply when she saw Dave wearing only a pair of boxer shorts as he stood at the stove frying bacon and eggs.

She'd always loved his body. It was long and muscular. Dave had never fixated on muscle-building and the like, although he had always jogged and worked out enough to stay in shape. Other than smoking a few joints in college, he didn't do drugs or smoke cigarettes. Nor did he ever indulge himself excessively with food or alcohol.

Now his body appeared to be in even better condition. His muscles were tighter and looked larger. Trish felt the stirrings of arousal, recalling what it was like to be in his arms with that long, muscular body pressed against her.

Don't go there, Trish. He's not ready for it yet.

She hurried into the utility room and threw all the wet clothing and towels into the washer. Checking the dryer, she removed his clothes and carried them out to him.

"These are dry now. You'd better put them back on before you catch a cold."

He looked at her and grinned. "Thanks."

Trish avoided looking at him when he pulled on the jeans and shirt.

"Sit down," he said, when he finished. "I figured you were as hungry as I was. This was all I could find. I think we really ought to get some food in this place."

"I agree. If you recall, I had just barely moved back in here, and I hadn't anticipated overnight guests. Maybe when it stops raining, we can go shopping."

"I just talked to the Agency. Bishop told me we should lay low."

"For how long?"

"I imagine until this mall thing settles down. We'll have to go in and give the police our statements. I also talked to Kurt. The woman's accomplice got away."

"Well, whether this mess is resolved or not, on Monday I have a painting crew coming in."

"I'd cancel that until things quieted down."

"And what about my luncheon date with Deb today?"

"Cancel."

"Really, Dave, do you expect me to stay caged up in this apartment until McDermott is caught? I thought we were to be out and around purposely to draw him out."

He put a plate of eggs and bacon down in front of her. "Eat, Trish. Then we have to talk."

It seemed so natural to be sitting across a table in their kitchen.

She and Dave had been together for six months; she and Robert had lived there together for the same length of time—even though she'd quit sharing a bed with him. But she still thought of this as *their* kitchen—hers and Dave's. She took a long look at him. And it will be again, my love.

"Speaking of painters, what color do you think I should use in the living and dining room?"

He shrugged. "That's your call. You're the interior decorator."

"It never hurts to hear another person's opinion."

"I always liked the beige look when we were together. It was calming after a hard day. This black-and-white deco look is a bit too extreme for my tastes. I'm not sure whether that long wall in the living room is a checkerboard, but I'm certain the design on the wall in the office is for playing tick tack toe."

"The whole look is another reflection of Robert's screwed-up psyche."

"Don't tell me you or Deb did this."

Trish giggled. "Deb disliked him enough to do it to him, but he had some woman he was sleeping with at the time do the decorating. When I saw it for the first time, I figured it must have been her revenge."

"There must have been somebody who liked the man."

"My dad came nearest to being the only one I know of. Tom Carpenter loathed him. He almost threw a punch at Robert shortly after we were married. Can you imagine? Pleasant, easygoing Tom.

"We'd had the Carpenters over for dinner one night and Robert suggested we play a game of wife-swapping." She shook her head in disgust. "Robert was so depraved. Why do you think I insisted upon separate bedrooms?"

"He sounds like a guy who wouldn't let a closed door stand in the way of what he wanted," Dave said, his expression tight.

"A closed, *locked* door," she corrected. "But actually, it didn't matter to him. I told you we didn't marry for love. He had a harem of women at his disposal and said I was no great loss. He said that I was cold and unresponsive, and having sex with me was like making out with the walking dead." She half smiled. "I don't have to tell you that the term he used for *making out* was considerably more crude."

A long silence prevailed before he asked solemnly. "Why did you even remain here, Trish?"

"Dad had a long talk with Robert and convinced him

to go into therapy. He told me the least I could do was support him for the effort, and accused me of still mooning over you and not giving my marriage a fair chance to succeed. I admit I couldn't bear to have Robert touch me, so I figured I did have to accept some of the blame."

"And did the therapy help?"

"Oh, yeah," she scoffed. "He flaunted his female friends in public more than ever. He even started to bring them here at night."

"So you moved back home."

She paused and gazed into space as she dredged up that painful memory.

"I'm sorry, Trish. Forget it. It's none of my business," Dave said.

"No, I want to tell you, Dave. I've kept it inside too long as it is. I didn't even tell Deb or my Dad the full story."

"Then why tell me?"

She didn't know why herself. But she knew if they were ever going to get together again that it was important he understood all there was to know about her relationship with Robert.

"The morning after one of Robert's humiliating public displays—this time with two prostitutes he'd hired for the night—I decided I couldn't take another moment of it and was packing to leave when he came home. We had a tremendous quarrel and I told him the therapy wasn't working and I was going to file for divorce."

She closed her eyes, reliving that horrendous scene. "He turned violent and began to hit me and call me every foul name he could think of. Then he hit me so hard that he knocked me off my feet and I struck my head against his damn metal safe. I was so dazed, I couldn't move, and that's when he…when he raped me."

A nerve jumped in Dave's cheek. "Did you have him arrested?"

She snorted. "Where have you been, Dave? Conjugal rights, you know—a wife has to have a lot of evidence to prove her husband raped her. And it's pretty hard to say no when you're too dazed to speak or move."

"You said he hit you. Didn't you have bruises to prove it?"

"And he could say I fell. Then it becomes a he-said she-said situation. Besides, Robert threatened that if I called the police or tried to divorce him, he'd see that my father spent the next twenty years in prison."

Dave's eyes glowered with rage. "And what did Henry do when you told him?"

"Dad had been out of the country when it happened, and by the time he returned my bruises were pretty well faded. I didn't tell him about the rape. And as I mentioned before, he asked me—for his sake—not to rush into any divorce, because if Robert carried out his threat it would only stir up old ashes that would harm the reputation of the firm.

"Later, I had my doctor examine me and the medical tests confirmed that I was neither pregnant nor HIV positive."

She lowered her eyes to avoid looking at him. The whole situation was so humiliating.

"I'm not a heartless bitch, Dave. I hope you understand now why I cannot bring myself to mourn Robert's death."

"Trish, I know you're not heartless, and I know how our breakup affected both of us."

He reached across the table and squeezed her hand. "And, lady, I don't know where Robert Manning was coming from but you're not cold and unresponsive. I've never known a woman as responsive as you."

She glanced up at him sheepishly. At the warmth in his eyes, a quivering smile tugged at the corners of her mouth.

"Really?"

"Really. There's something else we have to discuss. I had hoped to keep this from you, but the incident in the mall forces me to tell you. Let's go into the living room and sit down."

Once seated, her previous remorse had shifted into a look of apprehension. "What is it, Dave?"

"Your father told me last night that McDermott contacted him."

She bolted to her feet. "What!"

"I'm quoting him, Trish. This is not only the Agency's theory anymore."

"Why would McDermott contact my father?"

"Because he knows Manning and your father were working together."

"Did my father admit to that, or is it some more of your theory about him?"

He grasped her by the shoulders and stared into the anger and hostility that had replaced the previous anxiety in her eyes.

"Trish, listen to me. I don't intend to turn this into a dispute over your father's guilt or innocence. That's an issue you'll have to face and deal with. He said that McDermott accused him and Manning of double-crossing him, and, according to Henry, McDermott admitted killing your husband."

"It's not true. I won't believe it. Don't keep saying it, Dave. Please, don't keep saying it," she pleaded in a wounded whimper.

Her control was so tenuous, her anguish so unmasked, that his heart ached for her. With all that had happened in the past week, how could she keep taking these blows and not stay down for the count?

He pulled her into his arms and held her tightly, hoping that his body could absorb some of her pain. When he felt her still shaking he lowered her back down on the couch and sat down beside her. Her hand trembled when he grasped it and held it between his own.

"Trish, I didn't want to tell you this, but the incident in the mall forces me to. Your father said that McDermott threatened to do the same to you as he did to Manning if Henry doesn't meet his demands."

"What demands did McDermott make?" she asked.

"He wants five million dollars—"

She jerked up her head with a hopeful gleam in her eyes.

"Well, don't you see, Dave, that's more like a ransom demand, not an indication that my father was involved with him. He knows my father is a rich man and is trying to get money out of him, that's all."

Dave released her hand and stood up. *God, Trish, will you ever face the reality about your father?*

"McDermott demanded your father return the diamonds, too."

Once again he had deflated her hopes. Kicked the legs out from under her. It showed in the slump of her shoulders and the lengthy silence that followed before she finally spoke.

"What did Dad say to that?"

"He said he didn't have the diamonds."

She looked up at him. "Do you believe him?"

Good job, Cassidy. You can be real proud of yourself. Go ahead. Finish the job that McDermott failed to do and drive the knife in deeper.

He cupped her cheeks between his hands. He

couldn't look into the probing hope in her blue eyes and lie to her.

"No, Trish, I don't believe him. I believe he's guilty as hell."

Call it sympathy, a need to comfort her, or just plain need to feel her in his arms. He did the dumbest thing he could think of—he lowered his head and kissed her.

He moved his mouth over hers, devouring their softness. They tasted so sweet. So damn sweet.

She parted her lips, and he savored that unforgettable taste of Trish and the incredible feeling that shut out everything except their need for each other. His tortured soul had hungered for it as much as his body had done and he crushed her tighter against him.

The harsh drone of the buzzer broke them apart. For the longest moment they stared in bewilderment at each other, then he released her.

"That must be Deb," she murmured in a confused voice. "I called her and explained the situation, and she said she'd come over here for us to talk."

"Good idea," he said. "It will help you to pass the time."

The conversation had become ludicrous. "Will you entertain her while I get dressed?" She hurried into the bedroom.

"Well, finally!" Deb groused when he got on the intercom. He buzzed her in and returned to the kitchen and poured himself another cup of coffee.

This time he'd really fouled up the situation.

Dave and Deb chatted over coffee until Trish joined them. She had changed into a halter top and a pair of shorts. She looked great. As long as they were confined to the apartment, those long, tanned legs of hers sure made a great view.

He noticed that Trish had composed herself, too, and showed no signs of the effects from their kiss or conversation—but he couldn't help but wonder what was going through her mind.

To pass the time he washed the dishes and cleaned up the kitchen, then he went into the den and watched television while the two women went over some business arrangements.

Before leaving, Deb came in to say goodbye.

"Take care of her, Dave," the usually blithe woman said somberly.

"Nothing's going to happen to her," Dave said.

"You won't let it happen, I know. You two darlings haven't fooled me for a moment. I can sense that things still aren't the same between you and Trish, but I have faith in both of you. I know you'll work it out."

She kissed him on the cheek. "I'm glad you're back, darling. So glad you're back."

"Say hello to Tom for me," he said as he showed her out.

"We'll have to get together for dinner. How about next Saturday night, our place?"

Dave nodded. "Sounds good. I'll check it out with Trish."

That would be a week from now. He didn't say that by next Saturday he might not be around. That he hoped McDermott would be in custody, and for all Dave knew the squad could be in the Middle East or some other dangerously exotic location. He didn't tell her that by next Saturday he might have said goodbye to Trish again.

"So did you and Deb settle your business?" he asked when he rejoined Trish.

Trish's eyes gleamed with enthusiasm. "Yes, I'm excited about a new project we're about to start. A complete renovation of a fourteen room Victorian."

"You never said what your father thought of the idea of you and Deb going into business."

Her smile faded. "He thought it was just a passing fancy with me."

"Is it, Trish?"

"I think our record speaks for itself. I'm a little disappointed, Dave. You sound as if you have as much confidence in me as he did."

"Not at all. I believe you can accomplish any objective you put your mind to."

That was how she'd always felt about him, too. Had been part of the beauty of their relationship. A deep camaraderie between them. Dave had always been supportive of anything she did, and it had always added to her confidence.

In addition to which, they enjoyed the same kind of food, books, movies and television shows. They shared the same religious and political beliefs.

But the undeniable thing they had in common was the sheer pleasure of just being together. Whether having sex or just hanging out, they enjoyed each other's company.

The only issue between them was her father. And it had proven to be one too enormous to overcome.

Now, as she listened to Dave's words of encouragement, Trish smiled secretively.

He'd probably sing a different tune if he knew her new objective was him.

"Thank you, Dave. And you'd be surprised about everything I have in mind."

A short time later, Kurt Bolen showed up with a couple of decks of cards and a board game Dave had told him to bring. Dave made out a grocery list for him to fill, and along with the groceries, Kurt brought back pizzas for them to eat.

When Kurt prepared to leave, Dave told him to inform the rest of the squad they could take the night off because he and Trish were housebound. So, shortly after Kurt's departure, once again she and Dave were on their own.

Which again created an awkwardness. The kiss they had shared was foremost on both their minds. Finally Dave broached the subject.

"I'm sorry about the kiss, Trish."

"I'm not," she said, unable to deny the truth. "It was a very tender gesture, Dave, so there's no need for you to apologize."

"I still shouldn't have kissed you. You're very vulnerable right now."

"Look, I understand why you did it, and I'm not reading any more into it than a compassionate gesture from a friend. The important thing is that we *are* friends again."

"I'll always be your friend, Trish, I won't try to deny that I've been bitter over our breakup, and I've tried hard to resent you. But I can't. Whatever the reason we're unable to make it together, it is not of our choosing."

His chuckle was deep. Throaty. Its warmth carried to his eyes.

"Lord knows, if loving was all it took, it would have been a slam dunk for both of us."

The laughter left his eyes, but his tone remained gentle.

"But it would destroy us to try to pick up where we left off, Trish. The kiss was a mistake, so we'll both be better off not to let it happen again."

Trish smiled and turned away.

But it will, David Cassidy. And whether you admit it or not, you want it to happen as much as I do.

Dave cleared his throat. "When are you bringing Ayevol over?" he asked in a light tone to change the subject.

She sat down beside him on the couch. "As soon as the painters are done and I have the place entirely in shape. It should be in another week."

"You know what a great watch dog he is?"

"Yeah, right. Even a kitten would be better protection."

His laugh was infectious. "He's just a trusting little guy. He loves everyone."

"He sure didn't love Robert."

"He was just responding to your vibes," Dave said. "You know how empathetic dogs are."

"Remember the time we went camping and the grass snake he was sniffing out bit him on the nose. He scooted back to us on the double," she said.

"Or what about the time we were visiting Kim and after Ayevol gave her cat his usual enthusiastic greeting and turned to walk away, the damn cat hissed at him and jumped on his back."

"And Ayevol stayed on your lap for the duration of the visit," she said.

They both broke into laughter.

"Yeah, I missed that little guy."

"He missed you, too, Dave."

That shared reminiscence set the mood for the rest of the day.

The hours passed swiftly. They played several hands of double solitaire and then switched to a game of Scrabble, before they finally settled down to watch television.

The evening news came on and covered the events of the shooting in the mall and made reference to a mysterious couple who fled the scene.

"Who do you suppose that could be?" Dave asked, tongue-in-cheek.

"I can't imagine," she replied.

Trish was pleased. They had fallen into their old relaxed banter. And naive as it might be, despite all the serious issues such as McDermott and her father's situation that still remained to be resolved, Trish was more encouraged than ever that she and Dave would work through their problems.

After another hour of viewing, Dave fell asleep. Trish felt the rumblings of hunger and got up to see what she could prepare for dinner.

Checking out his and Kurt's selections, she came to the conclusion that bachelors should not be allowed to prepare grocery lists. She narrowed the possibilities down to macaroni and cheese or broiled steaks and frozen French fried potatoes—which actually would have to be oven fried because Kurt had failed to purchase any cooking oil.

She was in no mood for a heavy meal of steak and potatoes, but Dave might be. She went back to the den to ask him.

He looked so peaceful asleep that she hated to disturb him as she shook him lightly on the shoulder.

"Dave, what do you want for dinner: steak and potatoes or mac and cheese?"

"Whatever you want, angel," he said drowsily, and went back to sleep.

Smiling, Trish went into the kitchen. He had called her angel. His affectionate nickname for her. First the kiss and now the nickname.

Yes, it was only a matter of time before he'd break down completely.

Trish began to hum as she prepared a tossed salad.

Chapter 11

"So what's it going to be?" Trish asked when they'd finished dinner and the dishes. "Television or Scrabble?"

"I've been thinking about this whole McDermott situation. Obviously he doesn't have the diamonds or he wouldn't still be trying to kill you."

"So who do you think has them?"

"I figured your father. But if so, there'd be no reason for him to tell me about McDermott's phone call and threat on your life."

"So now you think Dad was telling you the truth," Trish said hopefully.

"Only about not having the diamonds. He implied he got involved with McDermott for the excitement of it. I don't think he'd risk your life over money and diamonds."

"Gee, Dave, that's the kindest thing I've ever heard you say about him. Is this an admission that you were wrong about him?"

He shot her a cold-eyed glare. "Not likely, Trish."

"Well if Dad doesn't have the diamonds, Robert must have given them to someone."

"That's what I'm thinking. A close friend, maybe."

"I'm not exaggerating; I truly believe he didn't have any close friends."

"How about a girlfriend? Do you know who he was sleeping with lately?"

"Anyone, as long as his money held out."

"This is no time to be cynical, Trish. Can you come up with a name?"

"Dave, my only guess would be his secretary, Sharon Iverson. I think he trusted her. I know they had a brief affair, and he didn't fire her when it was over so they must have stayed on good terms."

"Do you know where she lives?"

"Not exactly. I vaguely remember mailing her a wedding invitation, but that was two years ago. The address had a tree in it. Pine Ridge or Oak Grove. Something like that."

Dave stood up. "Where's the telephone book?"

"In the drawer of that end table."

Dave quickly paged through the directory. "There's an S.D. Iverson listed on Willow Ridge."

"That must be it."

He quickly dialed the number and the ring was answered with a throaty, "Hello."

"Miss Iverson?" he asked.

"Yes."

Dave gave Trish a thumbs-up. "Miss Iverson, I'm with the insurance company investigating the recent death of Robert Manning. I wonder if you would answer a few questions for me."

There was a long pause, then the velvet voice replied, "I don't think I can be of much help to you, Mr.—"

"Webster. Dan Webster," he said quickly, glancing at the dictionary lying next to the Scrabble board. "You were Mr. Manning's private secretary, weren't you?"

"Yes, but I've told the police everything I know."

"If it wouldn't be too inconvenient, I'd like to hear it for my records."

"Are you the person who just called and hung up?"

"No, ma'am."

"Very well, Mr. Webster. Come to the office tomorrow morning and I'll speak to you then."

An uneasy feeling began to gnaw in his craw like it did on a mission when he sensed something was going awry. He was convinced more than ever that he had to talk to her as soon as possible.

"Miss Iverson, would you object if I came over now? I'm short on time and I could type up my report tonight and be out of here in the morning. It shouldn't take longer than thirty minutes."

He could hear her sigh of impatience. "I'm sorry, Mr. Webster, but you caught me practically on my way out the door. I'll be happy to speak to you in the morning. And be certain you have the proper identification, sir, or I won't answer any of your questions."

"Of course. I understand. I'll see you in the morning."

"Why did you lie about your identity?" Trish asked, as soon as he hung up. "Sharon would have seen you at Robert's service."

"That doesn't mean she would know who I was," he said.

"Perhaps not, but we made quite an entrance, Dave, and she'd have to have guessed that you weren't just your friendly insurance agent offering sympathy."

"I can be charmingly convincing when I want to be," he said.

"Tell me about it," she murmured in defeat.

"I'll call Kurt and ask him to get over here quickly to keep an eye on you while I'm gone. Do you have a flashlight?"

"Where are you going?" she asked, and went into the kitchen to get him the light.

"I'm hoping she wasn't lying about going out. I want to take a look around her apartment. Maybe I'll get lucky."

"Give Kurt a break. He's probably out on a date by now. I can come with you."

"You're safer here."

"Dave, my car is in the garage. I'll duck down in the seat when you drive out and if anyone is watching the building, he'll think that I'm still here."

It wasn't a bad idea. Even though Mike had said to lay low, that gnawing in his craw was causing Dave a sense of urgency.

He checked his gun, and slipped it into the leg sheath. "Okay, let's go."

The earlier rain had freshened the air but the humidity was a killer.

Trish huddled on the floor of the front seat as they drove away. Glancing in the rearview mirror, Dave noticed that a car pulled away from the curb, but it was too dark to read the plate or determine the make of the car.

"Stay down. If we're being tailed, we didn't fool anyone."

When he had to stop at a light in front of a brightly lit strip mall, Dave got a good read on the car and license plate behind him.

In a short time he located the address he was seeking. A single streetlight on the corner cast a faint glow on a row of side by side condos in the sparsely populated area. Dave pressed the buzzer of Sharon Iverson's unit several times, and when there was no answer he pulled a key card out of his pocket and slipped it between the lock and the frame. After several attempts he succeeded in tripping the lock.

"Was that part of your CIA training, Agent Cassidy?" Trish asked, still trying to shake out the numbness from her cramped muscles.

"It has just occurred to me that if we're caught doing this, the Agency will be blamed."

"Don't you guys always get the blame anyway?" she said.

"Lately the press and the powers that be have taken some of the heat off us. The FBI is the whipping boy these days."

"This is an invasion of privacy, Dave."

"So is terrorism," he said, and opened the door.

He swept the room with the flashlight. "Let's make this fast because I have no idea where she went. She could come back at any time. And don't disturb anything," he warned. "We'll check out the end tables and drawers in here first. Maybe Manning had one of those fancy safes made for this place, too."

She started to cross the room and cried out and fell when she tripped over something on the floor.

"We could do this faster if we turned on a lamp," she complained.

"Are you hurt?" He offered her a helping hand to pull her up.

"Just my dignity."

Dave moved to a table and switched on a lamp.

"Trish, you're bleeding." He wiped the blood on his hand on his jeans and turned to her.

Trish was staring horrified at the body of a woman on the floor.

"Oh, my God!" He knelt down for a closer look. "Is it—?"

"Sharon Iverson," she murmured through the lump in her throat that had begun choking her. "Is she… dead?"

Dave nodded. "Her throat's been cut." He stood up and pulled out his cell phone.

"Hold it, pal, and get those arms up in the air," a voice declared.

Dave recognized the voice at once and raised his arms. Trish was still too shocked to obey the command.

"Arms up, lady," the speaker demanded.

Stunned, she turned around and faced the two men who stood with drawn pistols in the doorway.

Detective Joe Brady walked over to Dave. "Let's have that weapon you're holding."

Dave handed him the cell phone.

"It's a phone," Brady said.

"Yeah, be careful. It might go off any time," Dave said.

"Save your jokes for someone who appreciates them," Brady said.

"I was just about to call the police," Dave explained.

"Yeah, right," Brady scoffed.

Brady cuffed him while MacPherson put in a call for the coroner and CSU.

"This is ridiculous," Dave complained when Brady began to frisk him.

The detective gave Dave a snide look when he removed the 22-caliber pistol Dave wore in a holster under his pants leg. Then he handcuffed Trish.

Dave had long recognized that MacPherson was the more reasonable of the two men, so he appealed to him.

"Look, Detective MacPherson, you know as well as I that we just got here. I knew you were tailing us. I made your car when we stopped at the red light at that strip mall we passed."

"You still had time enough to kill her," Brady accused, after examining the corpse.

Brady's stupid belligerence was becoming exasperating. "Right. I cut her throat with my cell phone."

"Who is she, Cassidy?" MacPherson asked.

"Robert Manning's secretary."

MacPherson flipped through the small notebook he carried in his pocket. "Sharon Iverson. Thought she looked familiar."

"Yeah, but she wasn't wearing a red necktie then."

Trish gasped aloud at Brady's insensitive joke. "May I sit down?"

"Certainly, Mrs. Manning," MacPherson said.

Dave cast a worried look at Trish. She appeared quite pale. This was the second violent incident she had witnessed that day, along with the threat of almost getting killed herself. How much longer could she shrug off the effects from such crimes?

"Detective, Mrs. Manning has witnessed a lot of brutality today. Is it necessary to keep her cuffed?"

The two detectives exchanged glances, then MacPherson tossed the key to Brady. He went over and unlocked her handcuffs.

"Don't think I'm doing the same to you, dude," he said to Dave. "You two ain't fooling me one bit."

"I believe you, Brady. No one gets up early enough to be able to do that."

"You've got that right, Mr. CIA."

The emergency vehicles arrived, and, as he and Trish were being led away, a woman from the crime investigation unit stopped them. "Hold up. I want to get a sample of their DNA."

"You've already got our DNA on record," Dave said, "and you're going to find more of it again on the victim. Mrs. Manning fell over her in the dark, and I checked her for a pulse."

"I'd like a fresh sample taken at the crime scene," she said.

The CSU officer quickly took a saliva sample from each of them.

Once at the station, Brady and MacPherson interrogated them and took their statements as well as the ones relating to the earlier mall incident. By that time, Dave's call to Mike had gotten results, and he and Trish were released.

The two detectives drove them back to Trish's car. MacPherson shook hands goodbye. Brady merely scowled.

"I don't get it," Joe Brady said as they watched Cassidy and Patricia Manning drive away. "The two of 'em are doing each other; we find Manning in an alley with his throat cut and she's married to him; a woman's shot in the mall, and Cassidy admits he did it in order to save the Manning woman. Now there's another victim and guess who we find standing over the body? Geez, Wally, when are you going to admit I'm right? Anybody else would be busted and strapped to the hot seat by now, but both of them get a walk."

"So?" Wally asked, climbing into their car and sliding behind the wheel.

"So when are we putting that guy behind bars where he belongs?"

"Joe, you've got Cassidy pegged wrong. He's a hero. Him and his squad just got back from saving some American's life in one of those Banana Republics."

"Where'd you hear that?"

"His boss, but it's classified information, so don't go shooting your mouth off about it."

"Well, just because he's got a dangerous job, it don't mean him and his girlfriend are innocent."

"And just because he's her boyfriend and she was Manning's wife don't mean they killed anyone. We've got to stop concentrating on them and start paying attention to other suspects."

"Other suspects! How can we? They get knocked off before we get near 'em, thanks to your two lovebirds."

"I think we should pay closer attention to old man Hunter. I've got a hunch he's not as clean as he'd like us to think," Wally said.

"Yeah, well if that's so, we better check him out before he ends up dead, too."

Wally's curiosity showed heavily on his beefy face. "Don't you wonder, partner, why the CIA's so involved in this case?"

"'Cause one of their agents is a suspect?"

MacPherson shook his head. "No, I think it's more than that. I figure we've been barking up the wrong tree. I've got a hunch they're after the same guy that we are—but for a different reason."

"What makes you think that?" Joe asked.

"That business in the mall today. Kind of coincidental those guys happened to be there the same time as Cassidy and the woman.

"Morning jog, my ass! Those guys were on a stakeout. Along with Cassidy. If the truth was known, I bet we'd discover they're all CIA. Probably on that same special ops team."

"You ever stop to think that maybe Cassidy was the one the CIA was checking out? Maybe the CIA is beginning to believe your fair-haired boy ain't as squeaky clean as you'd like to believe," Brody countered.

"In your dreams, pal. They're all in it together. There's something going on here that's a damn sight more than the local murders of Manning and his secretary. If the CIA's involved, it's got something to do with national security."

"I still think Cassidy and the Manning broad are guilty as hell. The guy still had canary feathers hanging from his mouth when we released him.

"He says to me, 'It's not every day a person can count on two D.C. detectives as witnesses to his innocence.' I'm getting damn tired of Uncle Sam bailing this smart-ass out of trouble."

Wally snorted in amusement. "But the guy's right, Joe. You know as well as me, Cassidy didn't kill the secretary. And the more I see of that guy, the more I like him."

"Good. You can send him care packages when we finally lock him up."

"That's not going to happen, partner," Wally said, and wheeled the Crown Vic into traffic.

Dave pulled out his cell phone and called Kurt to clue him in on the latest development.

"What's all the noise about?" he asked, when Kurt answered.

"The guys and I are in a pool hall."

"Don't you guys get sick of each other's company?" Dave asked. "You all need to get a life."

"Like you don't," Kurt said. "So what's up?"

"Trish and I just left the police station. Robert Manning's secretary was murdered, and we happen to have found her body."

"You mean she was murdered at Manning's apartment building?"

"No, at her own."

"I don't get it. I thought you and Mrs. Manning were in for the night."

"It's a long story."

"I'd like to hear it. Why don't you join us at the pool hall and clue us in?"

Dave turned to Trish. "Too late to stop for a drink?"

"Why not? Anything's better than being holed up in that apartment," Trish said.

"Okay," Dave said to Kurt. "Where is this pool hall?"

"Pool hall," Trish remarked after Dave got off the phone. "I visualized a quiet bar, with soft music."

"I remember you used to be pretty lethal with a pool cue."

Trish chuckled. "Still am. Dad and I often shot billiards when I went back home to live."

"I might have guessed. That would take the expression 'behind the eight ball' to new heights."

"Not really, darling. I aced him the same way as I always did you."

"I'm going to make you eat those words, Patricia. It will give me great pleasure to wipe that smug smile off that face of yours."

"Just put your money where your mouth is, cowboy." Trish settled back with a contented smile.

A short time later Dave pulled up and parked in front of a corner bar with a neon sign spelling out the word *Pool* hung in the window. The loud blast of a rock band shattered the night when a couple came out of the door.

There were a dozen or more people at or around the bar. A couple of men were shooting pool at one of the tables and Kurt, Don and Justin were at the other. As soon as Dave filled the guys in on Sharon Iverson's murder, they resumed the pool game.

The stakes were ten dollars a game, and by the time Trish played each of them individually, she was forty dollars richer.

The crowd had thinned out at the bar, the other pool table was vacant, and fortunately to all concerned, the music had been turned down so that one didn't have to shout to be heard above it.

Don and Justin had moved to the bar and Trish was watching Dave and Kurt shoot a final game.

Dave glanced casually at the man who had just entered and took a seat at the end of the bar nearest the door. Leaning down to take his shot, he asked, "Make him?"

Kurt nodded. "Yeah."

Dave figured it best to get Trish out of there and saw that the hallway leading to the door marked *Women* was just a short distance away at the rear of the room.

"Trish, I want you to do exactly what I'm about to tell you," he said firmly. "Pick up your purse like all the ladies do, kiss me on the cheek and then go into the women's restroom. Lock the door and don't come out until I say you can."

"Why—?"

"No arguments, Trish. Do it *now*."

The man's arrival had not gone unobserved by Don

and Justin either. They made eye contact with Dave. Obviously, they had the same suspicions about the guy.

Trish threw Dave a confused look. "This has something to do with McDermott, doesn't it?" she whispered as she pressed a kiss to his cheek.

"We don't know, but we're not taking any chances."

"Okay, Agent Cassidy."

She walked away with a deliberate swing to her hips that drew every guy's eyes in the place except his and Kurt's.

Dave nodded to the two agents at the bar, then he reached down and pulled his .22 from the leg holster under his jeans. Kurt did the same.

When the suspect got up quickly and headed for the rear hallway, they followed.

"What's your hurry, pal?" Dave asked when they caught up with him.

The man spun around in surprise to find the four men holding weapons pointed at him.

"Now, real slowly, pal, back up to the wall and assume the position," Dave said.

The man did as told, leaned over, and put his hands against the wall.

"Why are you cops roustin' me? I ain't done nothin'," he whined.

If he took them for cops, Dave wasn't about to change his mind. "We're curious to know what you're up to."

"I gotta pee."

Don and Justin sheathed their weapons and began to frisk him. They came up with a wallet and a knife with an eight-inch blade.

Justin let out a long, low whistle. "What's this for, hotshot? To peel apples?"

"It ain't mine. I found it in a alley."

"Yeah, right," Kurt said. "And when you told the police they let you keep it because you have an honest face."

"I didn't tell the police."

Dave snorted. "I'd have never guessed. Let's see some ID."

He shifted through the wallet. There was nothing more than a driver's license, social security card and twelve dollars in it.

"Kind of far from home, aren't you, Mr. Harvey? This driver's license says you live in New York."

"I came here to find a job."

Even though the guy had dark hair and about a week's growth of beard on his cheeks, he bore a resemblance to the picture Dave remembered of Colin McDermott. After all, anyone could dye his hair.

"Dave, there's stains on this knife that look like dried blood," Don said.

"You cut yourself, Sean?" Dave asked.

"Yeah, when I found the knife."

"Knives can be real dangerous, Sean. How long have you been in D.C.?"

"Just got in," Harvey said.

"Where are you staying?"

"Ain't got a place yet. Figure maybe I'd get a room at that fleabag hotel a block from here."

"So you just wandered in here to take a leak."

"I came in to get a beer. What's wrong with that? You seen my ID. I'm old enough to drink."

"Like to believe you, Sean, but I think you had a different reason for coming in here," Dave slipped his gun back into the holster. "Let's go."

"Nobody's going anywhere until you tell us what's going on here."

The speaker was one of two uniformed police officers with drawn weapons who had suddenly appeared on the scene. The sound of a siren announced the arrival of another squad car.

"I can explain everything, officer," Dave said. The last thing they needed was interference from the D.C. police. "We're working undercover."

"You fellows aren't from our precinct. If you're making a collar, we'd like to see your shields."

"We aren't carrying them. I told you, we're working undercover."

By this time two more police officers had joined them.

"What's going on?" one of the new arrivals asked.

"These guys claim they're working undercover, but they aren't carrying shields. We'll have to take you all in. While we're waiting for the wagon, we'd like some ID, fellows," the officer said.

"No problem." Dave and the others handed him their wallets, along with Harvey's.

"Well, Mr. Cassidy, you appear to be the only city resident in this group. Your friends seem to come from all over, so I'm afraid I'll have to ask you all to get your arms up in the air while we frisk you. Lightly and politely, gentlemen," he added.

"Careful with that knife," Dave warned, when one of the officers took it from Don Fraser, along with his gun. "That's evidence, and you're compromising it. This man is a suspected terrorist."

"Terrorist! I ain't no terrorist," Harvey screeched. "I came in here to have a beer, and these guys came at me with guns."

"There are bloodstains on that knife that may connect him to a recent murder here."

"What murder?"

"Robert Manning's. That is if your fingerprints haven't obliterated the evidence."

"You guys sound more like feds," the offended officer said. "You figure you're the only ones who do things right. So which of you is Sean Harvey?" he asked, flipping open one of the wallets.

Disgusted, Dave shook his head. "The suspect."

"As far as I'm concerned, pal, you're all suspects until you prove otherwise."

He proceeded to have them all handcuffed and herded into the patrol wagon that had arrived on the scene.

"This reminds me of the good old days in Hoboken," Justin said. He was the only one who appeared to be enjoying himself.

"You ride in a paddy wagon before?" Kurt asked.

"Yeah, a couple times," Justin said, grinning. "Mostly for stealing cars for joyrides."

"Did you ever do time?" Don asked.

"No. Six months on probation, or public service like helping to clean up the streets. Small-time stuff like that."

Dave's mind was on the problem at hand. He'd have to call Bishop to get them out of this latest situation or the police would probably take mug shots and fingerprint them unless they revealed their true identities. This damn case was the biggest foul-up he'd ever experienced.

Physically this Harvey fitted McDermott's physical description except for red hair, but the terrorist was such a chameleon, who really knew his true color of hair? The guy's accent sure wasn't what he'd expected. But he'd probably perfected a dozen accents to go with his many identities. With any luck, the blood on the knife would tie him to Manning's murder and Trish would no longer be in—

Trish! Good Lord! In all the hustle he'd forgotten about Trish locked in the women's room. He'd told her not to come out until he said so. How long would it be before some woman would want to use the john? Then Trish would have to unlock the door.

He buried his head in his hands. A damn foul-up from beginning to end! He could only hope that they had McDermott. If they didn't, Trish could still be in danger.

Chapter 12

Trish glanced at her watch. She'd been in there for twenty minutes. Whatever Dave was up to, he must have settled it by now.

Someone came and tried to get in, then walked away. From the click of heels on the wooden floor, she could tell it had been a woman.

What was keeping Dave? Could he have been hurt? If so, surely one of the other guys would have come to get her.

After ten more minutes, someone came to the door again and tried to get in.

"Anyone in there?" a female voice called out.

"Yes," Trish replied.

"Are you okay, lady?" the woman asked.

"Yes, I'm fine now." She couldn't remain there any longer and opened the door. "I'm sorry. I was feeling nauseated."

"Anything I can do for you, honey?" the woman said.

"No, I feel much better now. Thank you just the same."

She was shocked to discover there was no sign of any of the four men in the pool hall. What was going on? She went up to the bar.

"Did you notice what became of the men who were playing pool with me earlier?"

"Yeah, the police hauled them away," he said.

"What?"

"Guess they were hassling some guy and pulled guns on him. How come the cops didn't run you in with them?"

"I really didn't know them that well," Trish said. She was beginning to become proficient at this cloak-and-dagger stuff. Lying was coming really easy to her.

"You came in with one of them."

"I met him outside."

He gave her a leery look. "You sure was cozying up to 'em enough. You ain't one of the working gals, are you? You look kind of familiar, but I don't remember seeing you around here before."

Trish had watched enough television to know he was referring to a prostitute.

In a deep, throaty voice she murmured, "I guess that would depend upon where else you've been, handsome."

Yep, she was really getting into the role. Trish winked and departed.

She hurried over to her car, parked in front of the bar, and rooted through her purse for her keys before she remembered that Dave had them. There would be no sense in trying to track him or his squad down. She was positive he would eventually get around to calling her.

And she sure had a bone to pick with him. Thirty minutes locked in the women's room of a bar was not her idea of a fun time. The least he could have done was take a minute to tell her to come out.

Seeing a cruising cab, she flagged it down.

As she drove away a man stepped out of the shadows and watched her depart. He went over to her car and peered inside it. The man glanced around the deserted street, found a hunk of rusty metal and broke the car window. Then he opened the car door and climbed in.

Her cell phone lying on the table was blaring Beethoven's Ninth when Trish entered the apartment. She rushed over to answer it.

"Where have you been?" Dave asked. He sounded rattled, which was entirely out of character for him.

"Where do you think I've been?" she said. "Just where you left me. Locked up in the women's room of that bar."

"I've been calling you for the past forty-five minutes. Why haven't you answered your cell phone?"

"Because I didn't have it with me. I'm home now."

"Dammit it, Trish, if you aren't going to carry it with you, why have one?"

She was the one who should be upset. Thanks to him, she had spent thirty minutes in that two-by-four, smelly room.

"Is that the question of the day, Agent Cassidy, or did you have a specific reason for calling?"

"I'm sorry. This place has got me frustrated. The cops pulled us in for questioning. How long did you stay in there?"

"A half hour. I finally had to open the door. The bartender told me you guys were hauled away by the police. So what happened with your suspect in the bar?"

"He claims he's just a migrant and has nothing to do with McDermott. The police are checking out his story."

"Do you think he's McDermott?"

"It's kind of a stretch. But he acted suspicious. Had a knife with dried blood on it. So it's hard to say. Could be a case of being in the wrong place at the wrong time."

"See, you should have kept me with you. I saw McDermott in Morocco. Who could forget that red hair."

"This guy has dark hair and a thick coating of whiskers. Of course McDermott's a master of disguise, so we can't rule anyone out. Anyway, we should be out of here shortly. We're waiting for Mike Bishop to get us released."

"Dave, I've been thinking about those missing diamonds. What if Robert put them in our storage locker downstairs? Who would even think of looking there?"

"Could be worth checking out, I suppose."

"I think I'll go down and look."

"Stay where you are. Gotta go now. Bishop just got our release. I'll be home soon."

"On your way here, stop and pick up my car where you left it. You have the keys. I had to take a càb home."

"Sorry about that. In the meantime, forget the locker. We'll check it out tomorrow morning."

"Okay," she said. "Bye."

Trish hung up the phone and headed for the bedroom. Doggone it! She'd forgotten about the locker when she packed up Robert's things. There were probably a lot more of his personal belongings down there.

But Dave was right. It would be better to wait until morning when she could pack them up.

But her curiosity was too piqued to put the thought out of her mind. Besides, the man the police had in custody undoubtedly was McDermott, so that danger was behind her.

And even if he wasn't, as long as she remained inside the building there was no danger. Dave was too paranoid. No one could get in without a key. There was a security guard in the lobby, and there were cameras on every floor.

Trish pivoted and went into the kitchen and dug the locker key out of a drawer.

The locker room was located on the parking level of the building. Each door of the lockers was as firmly secure as the apartment doors of the sixty apartments in the structure. Therefore, it was logical to Trish that Robert might have stashed the pouch of diamonds in the locker.

A couple from the third floor whom she had often met on the elevator or in the weight room when she and Dave were together, were just leaving the locker room when she arrived. They chatted for a few minutes while the two people expressed their pleasure to see she'd moved back in. To her relief, neither one made a reference to Robert's death.

When they'd departed, Trish entered the room and turned on the lights. The large, cavernous room was instantly flooded with bright light to reveal six aisles of ten lockers to a row. Signs hung from the ceiling above the aisles designating the floor number. Her locker was the last one at the far end of Aisle 5.

Trish had not been in the locker since she removed all her belongings a year and a half ago. To her delight the locker was practically empty except for a few scattered unsealed cartons that Robert had hastily dumped there.

She sat down and began to sort through them. One was a full carton of porno magazines. Those could go straight to the incinerator.

Disgusted, she moved on to the next box. It was full of clothes hangers and a discarded Walkman and tape. She switched it on and the cassette was an exercise tape. What he used that for, she hated to imagine. He'd always prided himself on getting his exercise in bed. Trish couldn't help recalling how amusing she'd thought the remark had been when she first met him—until she'd discovered what he really meant by it.

From what she could see the remaining cartons were clothes. Robert had always considered himself the Beau Brummell of the twenty-first century and had kept abreast of the slightest changes in men's fashions, however short-lived they might have been. Maybe she could donate them to a theatrical company—or a circus clown.

She had just closed up the last carton when suddenly the lights went out.

"Hey, the room's in use," she shouted. "Turn the lights back on." There was no response to her shout. Whoever had turned them off had moved on. Or had they?

Trish felt the rise of goose flesh when she heard a faint shuffle and knew she was no longer alone in the darkened room.

Kurt drove the rest of the squad home and Mike Bishop drove Dave back to the bar to pick up Trish's car.

"What the hell?" Dave said. "I know I parked it right in front of the joint." He got out of Mike's car and noticed shards of broken glass lying in the road where the car had been parked.

"That wasn't there earlier," he said to Mike. "Looks like someone might have broken a window and taken off with the car. I'm in enough hot water now with Trish. Wait until she hears this."

"Maybe she came back and got the car," Mike said.

"Could be, but it wouldn't explain the broken glass. Besides, I just talked to her about ten minutes ago. She made a point of telling me to pick up the car."

"Climb in, and I'll drive you home."

"I'm still staying at her apartment," Dave said. "Until we get a definite ID on McDermott, I'm not leaving her alone."

"Right," Mike said.

On the way there, Dave tried to reach her on the telephone. When there was no answer, he tried her cell phone.

He snapped the phone off. "She must be taking a shower."

"Or hasn't gotten back yet from picking up her car," Mike said, tongue-in-cheek. "She was probably pulling your leg the whole time. Most likely getting even with you for letting her sit for a half hour locked in the john."

"That wouldn't explain the broken glass," Dave said. "And, besides, I've got her car keys."

"Like she doesn't have a spare. Probably keeps it tucked in the same spot as her mad money. You've got a lot to learn about women, pal," Mike said, pulling up in front of Trish's apartment. "Anyway, I'll see you tomorrow at Sardino's unless Ann pops before that. She claims she won't. She doesn't want to miss the party."

"Okay, tomorrow night."

He waved as Mike drove away.

Dave stopped at the security desk to say hello to Ben Rose, the security guard who had just come on duty.

The old timer had been the guard there even before Trish and he had lived there.

"Ben, did Mrs. Manning go out a short time ago? She's not answering the phone."

"Saw her drive in about five minutes ago."

"Oh, thanks."

Mike was right, Dave thought as he rode up in the elevator. Trish was having a good laugh at his expense.

The lights were on in the apartment, and her purse and cell phone were on the kitchen table, but there was no sign of Trish. He even checked her bathroom. He called the security desk.

"Ben, did you say you saw Mrs. Manning driving in or out?"

"Driving in," he said.

"Did you follow her on the camera?"

"Not really. There was some action going on in the lobby that distracted me."

"Well, did you at least see her get out of the car?"

"Can't say that I did. Just saw her car pull in."

Dave's intuition had begun to buzz and his nerve endings began to tingle. "Okay, thanks a lot."

The whole thing with the car kept nagging at him. Something about it just wasn't right. He decided to go downstairs and check out the car.

Just as he suspected, the front window of the car had been broken, and a glance at the dash showed it had been hot-wired.

Trish hadn't driven the car back. But the person who did had used it as a ploy to get into the building. He probably intended to get out the same way, which meant he was still in the building looking for Trish.

But where in hell was she? She was either hiding from the guy or—

Recalling their last conversation it hit him where he'd find her. He could only hope he'd get to her before this intruder did.

Why hadn't she listened to Dave and stayed put in the apartment? Well she wasn't going to just sit there and wait for whoever was stalking her. Think, Trish, think. What can you use for a weapon? She could hardly strangle the intruder with one of Robert's dandy silk scarves. She had seen nothing that could be used to hit him with. She could try to poke him with a clothes hanger, but doubted it would be of much value in the dark.

Then she thought of the exercise tape. If she could create a diversion, she might be able to get to the door. Trish groped in the dark and found it. She'd given him a pretty good idea of her location when she had called out. Placing the Walkman at the door of the locker, she turned it on just loud enough to distinguish the low murmur of a voice, hoping that the intruder would think she was talking to someone.

Then she crouched low and cautiously sneaked over several aisles. Whoever was stalking her no longer attempted to be stealthy; she could hear him hurriedly approach the sound she made.

When she felt it was time to make her move, Trish stood up to make a dash for the door.

Suddenly she was grabbed from behind, and a hand clamped over her mouth. She had never figured there'd be two of them.

"Quiet," a voice warned in a whisper.

Trish ceased her struggle and looked up at Dave. She wanted to cry for joy, but his warning hand motioned her to silence. He indicated she remain crouched down, then slipped away.

Trish was petrified and didn't know what to do. She now was in Aisle 3, and if she ran straight up the aisle, she could reach the light switch and the door.

An eternity of heartbeats passed, then she heard a grunt, and then a thud. The sound galvanized her to action. She raced up the aisle and tripped the switch. The light flooding the room revealed Dave standing over the body of a man.

He was already on his cell phone.

Mike Bishop and the rest of the Dwarf Squad arrived at about the same time as the police squad. Dave had tied the man's hands behind his back with the cord from the Walkman. Trish walked over to them and stared at the bound man who had gained consciousness.

"That's him, Dave. That's the man I met at the home of Ali bin Muzzar."

Since McDermott had been apprehended by one of their agents, Bishop insisted McDermott was a prisoner of the CIA; since McDermott was a suspect in a local murder, the police claimed him. The feds eventually won the tug-of-war over the prisoner.

By that point, Trish didn't care who got McDermott, she just wanted them all to disappear.

Bishop came over and slapped Dave on the shoulder as they prepared to leave with the Irishman in tow.

"Great job, pal. We can handle the paperwork. You better stay with Mrs. Manning. She looks a little shaky."

"Really, Mr. Bishop?" Trish managed to tease. "I can't imagine why that would be."

"I think she's doing great," Dave declared in her defense. "I'm proud of the way she's stood up under it all."

"She did, indeed," Mike agreed. "And just to show

you my heart's in the right place, you and the squad can take the rest of the week off."

"You are so good to us, boss."

"That is unless some diplomat gets snatched," Mike added.

"Nothing personal, Mr. Bishop," Trish said, "but will you, your agents and your prisoner kindly get out of here. I hope I never have to hear the word *terrorist* again."

"We all do, Trish," Bishop said solemnly. "Sorry we had to make you a decoy."

"I wouldn't have missed it for the world. I really love you guys. It's just that there's so many of you, and you're all so big. I need some space."

She kissed Bishop on the cheek, and did the same to the rest of the team. "Good night, fellas."

"Dave, we owe this gal a big debt. Be sure and bring her to Jeff's birthday party tomorrow night so we can thank her properly."

"Good night, Mike," Dave said pointedly. He took Trish by the arm. "Let's get you upstairs."

Dave glanced worriedly at Trish as they rode up in the elevator. "You're right about needing some space, Trish. With McDermott in custody, there's really no reason why I have to remain here tonight. I could go back to my own apartment and sleep in a bed for a change."

"Not on your life, Agent Cassidy. If you want a bed, you can have mine. I have too many questions to ask you."

Without warning her legs suddenly buckled and she fell against him as they entered her apartment. Dave caught her to keep her from falling.

"Trish, what is it?"

"I don't know. My legs feel rubbery."

His arms were the most comforting feeling she'd ever known, and had thought she would never know again. Nothing could harm her as long as he held her.

And he did that until her trembling ceased.

"Are you okay now, angel?" he asked.

She knew as soon as she said yes she would lose that comfort, but she had no choice. She nodded, and he led her over to a chair.

"I don't know what happened. It came on so suddenly."

"It's reaction, Trish. It happens to all of us. I'll be right back." He left her and went into the kitchen.

"What are you doing?"

"I'm making you a warm glass of milk, then I want you to go to bed."

"I'm too keyed up to try and sleep."

He came back and handed her the glass. "Drink up."

Trish took the glass and took a sip of the warm milk in order to appease him.

"Question. Since he wasn't McDermott, who's the man you caught in the bar?"

"A migrant. Just as he said. Turns out the blood on the knife he had was his own as he claimed. The police are holding him, though. They figure he went into the bar to rob the place, so they're checking out databases for any priors."

"Why did you guys even suspect him?" Trish asked.

"His body language. When some people are up to no good they telegraph their intentions without realizing it."

"And what about McDermott? What kind of weapon did he have on him?"

"A knife."

"Oh, my God!" she murmured when the significance of it sank in. She swallowed hard and looked up with wounded eyes. "Do you think he would have used that knife on me, Dave?"

He couldn't look her in the eyes and deny it. He turned his head away.

"I admit I didn't take too kindly to having missed all the excitement in the bar," she said, "but maybe I should have remained there until you came and got me." Trish giggled.

Dave couldn't tell if she chuckled out of amusement or because her control was slipping.

"You always were a good sport, Trish. That's one of the characteristics I've always admired about you. You never pout to show displeasure like some women do, and you don't sustain anger like…" He lowered his eyes.

"Like what, Dave?" she asked when he didn't continue.

He couldn't meet the devotion in those trusting eyes of hers. She believed in him, and he wasn't worthy of it.

In the past, because of the unspannable chasm between him and her father, sometimes his love for her became an agonizing ache. He'd always wanted so badly to reach out and hug her. Hold her and comfort her as he had done just minutes ago.

"Like what, Dave?" she repeated gently.

"Like I do, Trish. I always was the one with the screwed-up psyche. Now how about you going to bed before the effect of that warm milk wears off?"

"Yes, doctor."

She came over and kissed him on the cheek. "Thank you for saving my life, Dave. Good night."

He watched her walk away. How he wanted to follow her into that bedroom. To lie beside her. He wanted her sexually, but mainly he wanted to hold her, to calm her fears and to tell her how much he loved her.

And that was the very thing he dare not do.

Chapter 13

"As soon as we finish breakfast, I'll gather up my things and get out of here," Dave said the next morning.

"I was hoping you'd hang around for a while." She grinned. "I've gotten used to seeing your scowling face across the breakfast table."

"With McDermott incarcerated, there's no reason for me to stay."

"Didn't Mike mention something about a party tonight?"

"Yeah. It's Jeff Baker's birthday. Ann and Mike are throwing him a party."

"Were you planning on going?"

"Yes."

"Alone?"

"No."

"Oh, I see," she said.

She hadn't thought of the possibility that he'd have a date. The whole time they'd been together he never mentioned another woman's name and she'd taken it for granted that he wasn't involved with anyone.

"Well then, I guess I'll have to go alone," she said.

"Trish, I intended to take you."

Joy surged through her straight down to the tips of her toes. "When were you going to ask me?"

"I had no way of knowing we'd have McDermott in hand, so naturally I figured I'd be covering you."

"Oh, I see. In the line of duty." It took some of the wind out of her sails, but any port in a storm right now.

"I'm excited. I haven't been to a party in ages. Guess I'll have to go home and bring over more of my clothes."

"It's not a ball, Trish. It's just a small get together at Sardino's."

"Sardino? Wasn't that the name of the man in the squad who was killed?"

"Yes. Mama and Angelo Sardino are Tony's parents. They own this small Italian restaurant. You'll love them."

"I'm sure I will. And just the same, I'm going home and getting something to wear. You don't have to come if you don't want to."

"I don't want to, but I'll come on general principle. I haven't officially been relieved of duty."

"Good, let's not waste any more time." She jumped up from the table and turned into a whirlwind cleaning up the dishes.

On the way they made a stop at Dave's apartment for him to get a suit, clean shirt and tie. Then they drove on to the Hunter home.

Trish was so excited she hummed as she looked through her wardrobe and selected a sleeveless black dress with a jeweled collar, black sandals and lingerie. No matter how Dave had proffered the invitation, they were going on a date again.

Rather than go inside and possibly confront Henry Hunter, Dave took Ayevol for a walk.

Upon returning to the apartment, he helped Trish empty the locker and haul away the cartons. Nothing remained of Robert Manning's belongings except some bold outlines on the walls, and the furniture, which a charity would pick up the following day. Before they knew it, the day had slipped away and it was time to dress for the party.

As Dave checked her wrap in the coat check, Trish heard the soft strains of a dance band above the drone of muted voices and laughter. Her gaze swept the room of the Italian restaurant, which had been closed to the public, and saw the familiar faces of the squad among the group.

A path opened up providing a view of Jeff Baker, Mike Bishop and a beautiful blond woman sitting at a corner table. Seeing Trish, Mike waved and beckoned to her to join them.

Dave returned and put a guiding hand on her back as they wove their way through the crowd toward the Bishops.

Dave had told her about Ann Bishop. The woman had been abducted by terrorists in French Guiana and Mike had led the squad that had gone in and rescued her and six-year-old Brandon Burroughs, the young boy in Ann's care. Mike and Ann had fallen in love and were married six months ago, and had legally adopted Brandon. They were expecting a child within three months.

Ann was warm and friendly, and she and Trish hit it off at once. What really surprised Trish was how the usually solemn Mike Bishop so openly adored his wife, and made no effort to disguise it.

The obvious devotion between the couple made Trish conscious of the obstacles she and Dave still had to overcome.

But we will overcome them, she vowed with a loving glance at Dave. Still she couldn't help envying Ann Bishop. The fortunate woman was carrying the child of the man she loved. How she wished she was carrying Dave's baby.

She didn't have too much time to lament that though, because the fellows on the squad kept her on the dance floor most of the time.

When the band began to play a slow tune, Dave turned to her and held out his hand. She slipped her hand into his, and he led her to the dance floor.

Dave was silent as they moved to the music. But he always had been whenever they danced. He preferred to concentrate on the music and always told her "one or the other, Trish. Dance or talk—but not both."

She stole a glance at him. His countenance was solemn and he appeared deep in thought. She arched a brow and began to tease him.

"I think I'm dancing a solo here. Earth to Cassidy. Come in, please."

Dave's eyes filled with laughter, and he grinned down at her. "It's a good thing you've got a pretty face because it sure has to make up for a wise mouth. So be quiet and enjoy the music."

He pulled her closer, and they yielded again to the rhythm of the music.

It felt so good being in his arms again. Natural. Where she belonged. Within minutes, she had become intoxicated by the male essence of him.

A vocalist began to sing an old Elvis Presley standard: the hauntingly sentimental lyrics about how one can't help falling in love.

Tell me about it; she had lived those lyrics. Trish snuggled closer to Dave.

She found it impossible to ignore his sensuality. The touch of his hand on her back was igniting her nerve endings, the pressure of his fingers was a tantalizing aphrodisiac and the scent of his aftershave a definite enticement. She was turned on.

She couldn't fight the overpowering need for him any longer. She stopped dancing and they halted on the floor. Raising her head, she looked up into his eyes and saw that they mirrored her own need.

"Let's get out of here," he said.

Within minutes, she was tucked securely in the front seat of his car. Dave didn't touch her or say a word. He drove, keeping his eyes on the road, his long fingers secure on the wheel. She wanted to reach out and cover his hand with hers, but she dared not. She sensed he was avoiding any physical contact in order to hold on to his control. She wasn't certain how much she had remaining herself.

It seemed like an eternity before he reached the apartment. The waiting had been intolerable. The moment he helped her out of the car, he pulled her into his arms. She became engulfed in an interminable kiss, spinning and twisting helplessly as she was drawn deeper and deeper into the depths of a swirling eddy.

She had no memory of how they reached her apartment. Once inside there was no time for subtlety.

Trish kicked her shoes away as Dave yanked off her wrap and threw it on a chair. Then he pulled off his jacket and tossed it aside. His shoes followed.

He wrestled impatiently with the knot of his tie as she pulled off her pantyhose, then she reached for him and tightened her arms around him, her fingertips caressing the corded column of his strong neck. She could feel the tautness that held his body in check, and slid a hand into the mahogany thickness of his hair. Its crisp springiness tantalized her fingertips.

His hands cradled the back of her neck and tipped her face to his. His kiss devoured her breath.

Attuned to the simplest touch, she closed her eyes as he pressed a kiss to each closed lid before claiming her lips again in another deep kiss.

Trish swirled in sensation when he began to rain quick, moist kisses on her face and mouth. Swept along by a torrent of long-suppressed passion, she felt his tongue lightly trace the outline of her mouth. Her hunger for him was insatiable—her body communicating this need with a mounting, pulsating response.

He nibbled at her mouth, then his tongue conducted darting forays into its heated chamber. She responded with a sensuous stroke of her hand down the sinewy column of his neck and into the open neckline of his shirt. She buried her fingers in the matted hair of his chest.

Her breathing became painful gasps when he slid his hand to her hips and pressed her against the intimate proof of his arousal, then captured her lips again as he unzipped her gown and shoved it off her shoulders.

Her breasts swelled under the heat of his gaze as his eyes clung hungrily to the sight of the skimpy black satin slip molded to the fullness of her breasts and soft curves of her body.

Shuddering with response, she gasped when his firm warm hands cupped her breasts and slid down her body in a slow, tantalizing examination of the glossy fabric.

Then, with a motion as smooth as the satin he fingered, he lowered the straps off her shoulders and pushed the garment past her breasts, his hands sweeping them in a caress as he did so.

Overpowered by the scent of him and the feel of the strength in the powerful muscles at her fingertips she pulled the shirttails out of his pants and released the remaining buttons of his shirt. As he struggled to free his long arms from the sleeves, she fumbled awkwardly with his belt in her effort to release it.

His name became a sensuous purr on her lips when his mouth closed around one of her breasts in an exquisitely rapturous suckling, then he captured the other in the cup of a hand and rasped the taut peak with his thumb.

She bit her lip to keep from crying out. Groaning with rapture, she abandoned her effort at his belt and pressed his head to her breasts.

His mouth continued to pay homage to them as his hand roved across the smooth plane of her stomach and stripped off her slip and panties.

Dipping her mouth to his shoulder, she sampled its saltiness with her tongue. The warmth of his hands slid to her rear and his fingers splayed across the sensitive nerve endings of her buttocks. Tremors raced down her spine when he filled his hands with the rounded cheeks.

Her head reeled with dizziness and she lost all hold on reality. She had no idea how much longer she could endure the erotic torture.

"I'm burning up, Dave."

"I know," he rasped hoarsely.

"Help me," she pleaded as the fire raging through her threatened to consume her.

"I will, angel. I will," he whispered in a hoarse assurance and pressed his hands more tightly into her silky flesh and lifted her. She curled her legs around him.

Smothering a groan against her mouth, he backed her to the wall and crushed her to him as he recaptured her lips. The kiss was too hungry to be gentle, her response as instinctive as breathing.

He carried her into the bedroom and laid her gently on the bed. Seconds passed like hours until the muscular warmth of him stretched out on top of her.

Trish had ached for this moment, and her body shivered with the thrill of it. How often had she tried to relive in memory the excitement his touch created.

He broke the kiss and swept her eyes, her cheeks, her neck with quick kisses that sparked that exquisite fire of passion wherever they touched. Breath was too precious to waste on words as he kissed her again and again. Rejoicing in the moment, she clasped her arms around his neck and clung to him.

He made an attempt to reacquaint his hands and mouth with her body, but their wait had been too long, the need too great to prolong it a moment longer. He entered her and their bodies clung and moved as one in the erotic harmony of lovers.

She cried out his name in ecstasy as they reached fulfillment.

As soon as his breathing returned to normal, Dave rolled off her and she shifted to her side and cradled her head in the hollow of his shoulder. She wanted to cry, but was too embarrassed to do so. It was the only way she could truly express the joy of being able to reach out and touch him again, to smell the intoxicating scent of him, the warmth of his muscular brawn.

His muscles were firmer than she remembered, obviously due to the strenuous military training. His flesh felt warm and tight beneath her fingertips. How she loved the feel of this man!

Despite his warnings, whatever future lay ahead, she would never stop loving him. And despite whatever denials or arguments he put forth, even if he wouldn't admit it, she knew he was as committed to her as she was to him.

They made love again, more leisurely this time as they rediscovered each other's bodies.

Now that his hands and mouth had a greater and freer access to her body, he explored her in an erotic probe. He had waited too long for this moment. He forced himself to execute control so that he could caress every crevice and hollow of her body with his hands and mouth.

She didn't have his control and was already aroused.

"Please, Dave. I can't take any more," she pleaded, her body arching against the moistness of his mouth when he closed it around a hardened nipple.

"The best is yet to come, angel," he murmured.

Raising his head, he stared down at her. Her dark hair was spread in dishevelment on the pillow, and he watched the changing expressions in her passion-heavy eyes as he began to stroke the heated chamber of her sex. He was helpless to resist the irresistible draw of it and lowered his head and nibbled the tender flesh of her inner thigh until he reached the throbbing source of her.

She began to writhe in wild abandon and her long fingers dug into the flesh of his shoulders as she clutched at him when her body started to shudder with spasms of erotic sensation.

The sight and feel of her arousal incited his lust. He

flicked his tongue across the swollen lips that protect-
ed that chamber, then shifted and once again plunged
his tongue into the heated moistness of her mouth. Her
tongue did an erotic dance across the roof of his and he
pulled away with a muffled groan into the perfumed
thickness of her hair.

She embraced him and her fingers swept the length
of his spine, hugging him against her own rounded
curves as her groping hands sought his hardened arousal.

"Please. Please," she groaned in heaving gasps, un-
aware of the havoc her searching hands were raining on
his body. Her breath became a quivering sob when he
raised himself and thrust into her.

"Dave!" His name escaped in a blissful cry that shattered the last vestige of his control.

His chest ached from the throbbing of his heart in
the long moments it took to restore his breathing to a
steady rhythm. He raised his head, cradled it on a
propped elbow, and stared down into the warm luster
of her deep blue eyes.

"We haven't lost it," she murmured in wonderment.

He grinned tenderly. "Did you think we had?" he
asked, and gently cupped her face in his hand.

Her eyes misted. "After six years I began to wonder
if it always was like this or just my memory torturing
me." She tenderly brushed back some strands of hair
from his forehead.

"Why would we ever lose it?" He settled back down
and pulled her to his side.

She sat up and leaned over him, her eyes beseeching
as she pleaded for his understanding.

"Dave, my marriage was the most dishonest thing
I've ever done in my life, and I'm not proud of it. For

the first time in years, I feel honest in a relationship. You make me feel that way, so I made up my mind I will settle for whatever you're willing to give me. And I still intend to do that. But I won't deceive you, Dave. I love you. No matter what I tried to tell myself to the contrary, I love you. I've never stopped loving you, and I'm old-fashioned enough to believe that you marry the person you love. You have his children. And that is my intent.

"I'll not ask any more of you than you're willing to give, I'll be content for us to be lovers to give you the time you need to adjust to the idea. But, David Cassidy, one of these days we *are* going to get married."

He pulled her down again against his chest and hugged her tightly for a few seconds. She responded with a drowsy yawn.

Dave rolled over, pinning her to the bed with his weight. For a long moment he stared down intently into her trusting and loving eyes.

"I love you, too, angel." Then he gently kissed her swollen lips.

He lay back again, cradling her head against his chest. Within seconds, her steady breathing told him that she had dropped off to sleep.

Unconsciously, he cradled her closer, pressing a kiss to the top of the tousled head that lay on his shoulder. His thoughts drifted to the passionate sex they had just shared.

From the time they'd met, they'd had great sex together. Always torrid, spontaneous and satisfying. Their separation and the events leading up to it had turned it this time into the most intense fulfillment they had ever shared.

But that didn't alter the obstacle that stood in the path of their marrying. How was he to convince her of that?

As soon as he was certain Trish was deep in slumber, Dave slipped out of bed and pulled on his shorts. Then he gathered up the rest of his clothing and the sheathed .22 he'd put on the nightstand when he had stripped. Grabbing a pillow, he left the room, closing the door quietly so he wouldn't wake her.

If he continued to lie there beside her, he knew he would reach for her again. He was finally free from the physical tension that had gripped his body for six years. That's what Trish could do to him. Whenever they had sex, it seemed as though their souls as well as their bodies became one—a mental as much as a physical effect on him. It had been that way from the first time he'd made love to her.

But this time it was different. His conscience cried foul. He'd misled her. By making love to her tonight, he'd given her a false hope that they could pick up where they left off. It couldn't happen. They would never know happiness as long as Henry Hunter stood between them. She was in such denial about her father that nothing he could say or do could change it.

He stretched out on the couch and closed his eyes. Time and time again he had challenged himself with the belief that maybe her accusation was true. Maybe it was jealousy or resentment on his part toward her father. If so, those were emotions that could be overcome rather than lose her. But they weren't the reasons he loathed the man. Henry Hunter purposely deceived the one person in the world who trusted and loved him unequivocally—his daughter. And when the truth was exposed, she would bear more shame and heartache over his guilt than that sonofabitch ever would.

And, regrettably, he would have to add to that heartache, because once again, he would have to try and make her understand that the reason that once had forced him to leave her still existed.

He fell asleep with that distressing thought on his mind.

Chapter 14

Trish kissed him awake. He opened his eyes. She was sitting on the edge of the couch leaning over him. Sunshine was streaming through the windows.

"Good morning," she said.

"Good morning."

He wove his fingers through the thick strands of her hair to lower her mouth to his. The kiss was slow and drugging, the kind of kiss that turns on your motor and waits until you shift into drive to see where you want to go with it. He found out when she took over the wheel.

Trish could do more with a kiss than any woman he'd ever known. Within seconds his groin was on fire and he had to have more.

He knew the pitfalls of making love to her again. It was rotten. Unfair to her. Would only make saying goodbye more difficult when the time came.

But good sex was like an avalanche, once it started rolling downhill it picked up speed, and there was no stopping it until it hit bottom—and sex with Trish was always good sex.

Besides, what better way to start off the day than getting rid of some sexual tension?

He rolled over and shifted her to her back, then resting on his elbow, he raised his head and looked down at her. She was breathing hard and her eyes were wide with expectation as she awaited his next move.

When they toppled off the couch her belted robe had parted enough for him to glimpse her nakedness beneath it. His hand stroked the satin flesh of her as he widened the gap in the front panels. For the briefest of moments he gazed greedily at the luscious, bountiful feast stretched out to appease his starved appetite. Breakfast time.

He lowered his head.

Later he stretched out his body. The firm floor felt good.

"Dave, wouldn't you rather go in and lie on the bed? It's much softer."

"I like it hard. It feels good."

"I like it hard, too." Then she chuckled delightfully and leaned over him. Her eyes were twin pools of devilment.

"Trish, I'm talking about the floor."

Her warm chuckle again caused him to grin. "You are shameless, woman." He tightened his arm around her and drew her closer.

Trish laid her head on his chest. "I have no shame where you're concerned, my darling. Do you know that the whole time you were gone I'd lie awake at night thinking about you. I told myself again and again that if only I'd known it was the last time we'd ever make love, I never would have stepped out of the shower that day we argued."

Her words were a grim reminder of what still lay ahead for them. He had to change the subject. He stood up and pulled her to her feet.

"You know, for two so-called intelligent people we've been pretty careless. We've had sex several times without using any protection. You're still on the pill, aren't you?"

"No, I haven't been since you left."

"Trish! You could get pregnant."

"Nothing would please me more. I want to have your child, Dave."

"My God, Trish, what about the danger of contracting—"

"Dave, I haven't had sex with any man except Robert, and that was two years ago. I had myself checked for any diseases when I left him."

"Did it occur to you that I could be a carrier?"

"I knew you weren't."

"I know I'm not either, but *you* had no way of knowing that."

She cupped his face between her hands. "Of course I knew. You're a man of conscience, my love, and if you were HIV positive—or had any social disease for that matter—you *would* have used protection. You're too honorable to have risked passing it on to me."

She narrowed her gaze and fought a smile. "Of course, that doesn't explain why you didn't use protection for your own welfare. You had no way of knowing whether or not I was infected."

He was saved from responding when her telephone rang. She stepped away to answer it.

Saved by the bell. What in hell could he say? He had no excuse. He'd always prided himself on having common sense and a level head. But nothing he'd said or done in the past couple of weeks made sense to him. He'd been running on high-octane testosterone—and the tank was full. He was so hot for Trish, he ended up doing just the opposite of what he'd warned himself not to do.

Trish had settled back in a chair and from her conversation he could tell she was talking to Deb, so he gathered up his clothes and headed for the shower. He shaved and showered, and when he finished and came back into the room, she was still on the phone.

He went into the kitchen and poured himself a cup of coffee and checked out the refrigerator—then settled for a bowl of cereal.

Trish came into the kitchen while he was eating and made herself a bowl of cereal and sat down opposite him.

"I'm meeting Deb in an hour."

"The two of you were just on the phone for a half hour and you're seeing each other in an hour. What's left to talk about?"

"We're meeting with clients who have a flight to catch in a few hours. They'll be out of the country for several months and want to go over some changes they want made in the house while they're gone."

She finished the cereal and coffee then rushed off to get dressed.

Dave cleaned up the kitchen and then put in a call to Bolen.

"You two sure left in a hurry last night," Kurt said.

"Yeah…ah, Trish wasn't feeling well, so I brought her home."

"Is she okay?"

"She's fine."

Dave had always been up front with Kurt, but at the same time he wasn't one to kiss and tell. Besides, he wasn't fooling anyone. Even though they never said so, he knew the guys on the squad had already figured out that much of the show of affection between him and Trish in public was the real thing. Dave made some small talk with Kurt then hung up.

Whoever said women took a long time to dress didn't know Trish. Within thirty minutes they were on the Beltway.

Showered and dressed, the same sensual goddess who had made uninhibited love to him on her living-room floor less than an hour previously, now Trish looked properly prim and efficiently professional dressed in a beige slack suit with her hair swept into a chignon at the nape of her neck.

While he…he was still feeling the aftershock.

The address Deb had given Trish was in Great Falls, Virginia, one of those high-rent districts not too far from D.C.

Once they turned off the highway, they had to follow a private circuitous road that wound through a heavily wooded area ending in front of a large, imposing house several stories high. It resembled a Victorian mansion. A for sale sign was driven into the lawn near the front of the house with the name and telephone number of a realty company. Deb's sports car was parked on the curved driveway.

"Well, well," Dave murmured, "the old homestead hasn't changed a bit."

"I love it," Trish said as she climbed out of the car.

"I can't wait to see the inside. I bet it's full of great nooks and crannies that are typical of many of these older homes."

Deb was engrossed in conversation with a well-dressed, grey-haired older man. While she was in the process of introducing them, Dave's cell phone rang and he stepped into another room to answer it.

"Dave, where are you?" Mike Bishop asked.

"In Fairfax County. Trish and her partner are with a client who wants his house renovated."

"Baker's calling in your squad."

"What about? I thought we had a week off."

"I don't know. Haven't seen him like this in a long time. He's in a big sweat. Something to do with the Mc-Dermott case, but he didn't tell me what. Only said to pull your squad in right away."

"Can't it wait?"

"Probably so, but Baker can't, so get in here on the double."

"All right. I'll round up the other guys."

"I'll take care of it. Pedal to the metal, pal."

Dave hurried back into the other room in time to hear Trish ask, "How long have you and your wife lived here, Mr. Phelps?"

"For about six months," Phelps replied. "We would have redecorated sooner, but we knew we were going to Europe for several months and thought it would be more convenient to hold off until then."

"That was a wise choice, Mr. Phelps," Deb said. "Redecorating can be very distracting."

Dave motioned to Trish. "Sorry to interrupt, folks. Trish, I'm sorry but I have to leave immediately."

"No problem, Dave. I can drive Trish back," Deb said. "We'll be through here shortly. Mr. Phelps has a plane to catch and his wife has taken the car and gone on ahead, so I promised to drive him to the airport."

"Okay. I'll call you when I'm through."

"See you later." Trish kissed him on the cheek. "Now let's go over the kitchen area, Mr. Phelps." She moved away with the man in tow.

"Deb, hold up a minute," Dave said, when she started to follow them.

"What is it, Dave?" she asked.

"If Trish has a problem call me on my cell phone. I have the same area code and exchange as Trish. The last four numbers are 9-8-7-6. They're easy to remember."

"What's going on?" Deb asked.

"Just being cautious. She's been through a rough time these past couple weeks. I'm waiting for the reaction to set in."

"You got the guy, right?"

"Yeah, I figure she's been living on pure grit until now. That's why I'm worried she's going to collapse. Sorry to rush away like this, Deb, but I've got to go."

"Don't worry, darling. I'll keep my eye on her."

As he climbed into the car, he glanced at the name and number on the for sale sign again. Why keep a stupid sign up on the lawn?

In the past Dave had always taken a logical approach to a problem. Granted, in the last couple of weeks since Trish had re-entered his life, his logic had been as effective as his good intentions. But as he wound his way back toward the highway something about this Fairfax County situation nagged at him.

Logically, anyone who had lived in a house for six months surely would have removed the for sale sign by now. And he knew women well enough to believe that most of them would hang around to discuss the remodeling of their new home.

Furthermore, why would a realty company even put up a sign on a house on a private road? Who would even see it? And even if they did, from what he'd observed in the past, once the house is sold they slapped a sold sticker on the sign, and removed the sign when the transaction was completed. Phelps had said they'd bought the house six months ago!

The puzzle pieces aren't fitting, are they, Cassidy?

Dave reached for his cell phone and punched in some numbers.

"Jan Kipling," a woman said pleasantly.

"Is this Kipling Realty?" Dave asked.

"Yes it is. What can I do for you?"

"How do you do, Ms. Kipling. I'm inquiring about a property you have for sale in Great Falls, Virginia."

"Oh, yes, on Walker Road."

"No." Dave gave her the street and address of the private road.

"Just one moment, let me check. No, I'm sorry, but that is not our listing, sir."

"Could you possibly have sold it within the last year?"

"No, sir. I've checked the record. We've never had a listing on that road. Let me check the Multiple Listing directory."

In a few seconds she was back. "Of course, I should have remembered. That property has been on the market for at least five years. The owners moved to Mexico."

"Your sign is on the front lawn of the property, Ms. Kipling."

"If it's our sign I think that someone is having fun at

our expense. We had a sign relating to the Walker Road property posted at the junction of Walker and River Bend roads. That's where many of the signs for Great Falls are posted. Property for sale on private roads will usually have signs posted at the foot of their private road. It would be very unlikely there would actually be a sign posted in front of the house. Perhaps some kids were fooling around, stole our sign and put it there as a joke."

"Thank you. I'm sorry to have bothered you."

Dave hung up the phone. So much for that theory. Some kids might have stuck the sign there last night for all he knew.

The damn road went on forever and forced him to slow his speed. He hit one of the curves too fast, spun around and almost plowed into one of the trees that lined the narrow road. The engine stalled when he tried to restart it.

Cursing, he got out of the car and in frustration kicked the tire. He was about to go under the hood, when he was blinded by a reflection from some near-by brush. He went over to it and discovered a concealed Jeep Liberty.

It wasn't an older, abandoned car. The Jeep was fairly new with a current license plate. What the hell was going on? It looked like the vehicle had been purposely stashed—concealed so it wouldn't be seen from the road.

At that moment his cell phone started to beep. Cursing, he reached for it.

"Yeah, yeah, I'm on my way," Dave grumbled into the phone.

"Baker just told me why he's up in arms," Mike Bishop said. "The prints of this guy we're holding don't match the ones we have on file for McDermott."

"But the guy looks identical to McDermott. So someone switched the fingerprints."

"Or it's not Colin McDermott."

"What are you saying?"

"Dave, I think Intel really blew this one. We just found out from the Brits that McDermott had a brother James. He disappeared about five years ago, and the woman you shot in the mall was Britany McDermott. She was married to James McDermott."

Dave tried to assemble all these facts as quickly as Mike fed them to him. "So, if the prints don't match, the man we're holding could be James McDermott."

"That's right."

"That still doesn't explain the exact resemblance unless…"

"You thinking what I am, pal?" Mike said.

"Identical twins," Dave said. "McDermott and his damn disguises!"

All at once everything fell in place. The sign. Deserted house. Dave's stomach knotted. "My God! Trish!"

"Where's Trish now?" Mike asked.

"I just left her. I had McDermott within arm's reach and I left her and Deb alone with him." He slammed the phone.

To hell with the car. He could make better time cutting across the woods than following the damn road.

He raced through the trees to get back to the house.

Trish loved the old house. It had three floors and her fingers itched to get at it and decorate it. She wished she had seen the house before the Phelpses had. Her mother had left her a sizable trust, and, not that she would ever need a house this size, but it was the very kind of home she'd love to own.

She climbed up to the third floor. There were four more bedrooms and two bathrooms. The house would definitely need new wiring, plumbing and heating, but the rest of the house was a decorator's fantasy. It had spacious, sunny rooms that could be transformed into a dream house.

The drone of Deb's and Phelps's voices carried up from below. Trish went to the railing to call to Deb to come upstairs.

They were downstairs in the foyer. She was about to call to them when she saw Phelps suddenly shove Deb into the hall closet and lock her inside.

Trish stifled a scream and ducked back. She sensed instantly that this had to have something to do with Colin McDermott. This was all a ploy to get her out here in this deserted area. And Dave and the squad were nowhere around.

Trish glanced around helplessly. The rooms up here were completely barren of any furniture. She had left her purse downstairs so she couldn't even call for help. As if any help could get here in time to do her any good anyway.

Whoever he was, he couldn't possibly know exactly where she was, but she didn't dare peek over the railing to see where he was or it might reveal her location.

His footfall sounded on the step, and she could tell he had reached the second floor.

Trish hunkered down and took a chance and cautiously peeked through the balusters on the stairway. Phelps's back was to her as he looked around and headed toward one of the bedrooms.

She could hear Deb pounding and shouting below, but Trish knew she could never get past Phelps to reach her.

Dammit! Quit calling him Phelps. He had to be

someone connected with that crazed McDermott. Or maybe he had escaped. If only she had her purse. Dave, what should I do?

In desperation she glanced out the window. It opened on to the roof, but she didn't know how she'd get to the ground. Maybe she could make him think she had escaped and he'd go looking for her, or maybe someone or something would cause a distraction and she could free Deb and escape. If only she had matches she could start a fire and trigger the fire alarm.

Right, Trish. Like this old house has a smoke alarm installed.

The open window would be her best ruse. Just as she raised the window, she heard him begin to climb the stairs to the top floor.

Dave, Dave, tell me what to do, she pleaded.

Then his answer came to her as clearly as a spoken word. "Go into the bathroom and lock the door."

She slipped out of her shoes. Praying that the floor wouldn't squeak, she picked them up and crossed the floor carefully.

The key was missing in the first bathroom she tried. Precious time was lost when she stole across the hall to the other bathroom. To her horror the key was missing from that lock, too. There was no time to go elsewhere. Nowhere else to hide. She closed the bathroom door quietly and looked around helplessly. She was trapped.

Trish pressed her ear to the door and forced herself not to scream—or to even breathe. The stealthy pad of approaching footsteps on the wooden floor was a more frightening sound than ponderous thuds would be.

It was stifling in the closet. Shouting and pounding on the door was accomplishing nothing except working up a sweat. Deb didn't know what was going on, but she knew Trish was in danger. That must have been why Dave had appeared worried when he left. But then, he would have insisted she leave with him.

The purse on her shoulder became a wearisome weight. She started to shove it off then paused. Of course! How could she have been so stupid? Waste precious minutes while Trish was in danger? Her cell phone was in the purse hanging from her shoulder.

Even in her distressed state, she had no problem remembering Dave's number. As long as one could count backward, 9-8-7-6 was easy to remember.

He sounded breathless when he answered.

"Dave, this is Deb. Phelps is a phony. He's locked me in the closet in the foyer."

"Where's Trish."

"She's upstairs somewhere. I heard him walking around above me. She must be hiding and he's looking for her."

"Deb, I'm almost there. The house is in sight. Call 911 and get some help out here."

"Okay, but hurry," she said.

Dave made no attempt to try to approach the house quietly. He wanted to make his presence known to the terrorist in the hope of drawing McDermott away from Trish before he could discover her hiding place.

"Trish!" he shouted when he entered the house. When there was no reply, he felt a rising panic. What if he was too late?

He halted long enough to turn the key on the hall closet and Deb came out looking frazzled but alive.

"Upstairs," she shouted. "I didn't hear anyone come downstairs yet."

Dave took the stairs two at a time. There was no sign of her on the second level, so he rushed up the next flight to the floor above and saw the open window. It had to be a ruse. No one could get off that roof without a ladder.

"Trish," he called out at the top of his voice. "Trish, where are you?"

His cry of desperation sounded hollow in the empty house. Trish wasn't there. By the time he had searched every room, nook and cranny in the house, the police had arrived.

They put out an all-points bulletin on the Jeep Liberty and license plate. While they continued to interview Debra, Dave returned to the site where he had left the car. Needless to say the Liberty was gone.

He put in another call to Mike, who had rounded up the squad and gave him an address where to meet them.

It turned out to be a rundown hotel. To Dave's surprise, Bishop had accompanied the rest of the squad.

"Britany McDermott's finally talked." Mike said. "She gave up Colin. Said he was staying here in room twenty-seven. It's your squad, Dave, so what do you want to do?"

That was Mike's way of letting him know he wasn't taking over. Dave was in charge. As soon as they found out the exact location of the room he gathered the men around him.

"Kurt, you and Addison go in through the fire escape. We'll give you two minutes to get into position. Fraser and I will go in through the door."

"What about me?" Bishop said.

"Sir, no disrespect, but I would appreciate your returning to your vehicle. This is a job for the team, not the Deputy Secretary."

Mike gave him a disgusted look and pulled out his weapon. "I'll pretend I didn't hear that."

"Okay, Bolen and Addison get going, Check your watches. Two minutes on the mark, then we're going in."

The two minutes passed like hours. Dave hadn't seen any sign of the Liberty on the street, and he held out little hope of finding Trish or McDermott in the room.

The desk clerk had implied he'd seen no sign of McDermott, but the terrorist would hardly parade Trish past the desk. On the other hand, the desk clerk could be an IRA sympathizer. The wall phone in the hallway indicated there were no phones in the rooms, but that didn't mean they hadn't worked out a warning sign if they were working together. The whole damn place could be a hotbed of terrorists.

Bishop's and Fraser's eyes never shifted from him as he watched the minute hand on his watch hop to the mark. He nodded.

The two men hit the door just as the window shattered inside the room. The door frame cracked and the door broke loose. Dave dashed in ahead of the two men and saw Bolen and Addison coming through the window.

Just as Dave suspected, the room was empty. A search produced several passports, wigs and other various components of disguise. Incriminating pieces of evidence but no clue where they could hope to find McDermott and Trish.

The fact that McDermott had snatched Trish and not killed her at the time was the only hopeful sign that he might be holding out for Hunter to come through with the money and the diamonds.

Even so, Dave felt that the cold-blooded killer would not hesitate to kill Trish once he got what he wanted.

"Mike, is there any information the CIA or FBI has

on this man to give us a clue where we might find him?" Dave asked.

"You know everything we do, Dave. His brother's clammed up and is not saying a word. His sister-in-law gave us this address. All the Agency can do is go back and squeeze them some more. I'm going back to Langley now and see what I can do from there."

Before leaving, Mike came over to Dave and put a hand on his shoulder. "I know how you feel, Dave. Keep the faith, pal. We'll find her."

Dave tried to figure out what to do next. The damn chameleon could be anywhere. The only probable link to the man was Henry Hunter. He was the only hope Dave had.

He dialed Hunter's office. His secretary informed him that Mr. Hunter could be reached at his home.

"You guys hang loose," he said to the squad as soon as he hung up. "I'm going to speak to Trish's father."

"Do you want company?" Kurt asked.

"Not now. I'm hoping I can get a lead from Hunter. I'll call you if I find out something definite."

Kurt nodded. "We'll go to Langley and wait for word from you."

Chapter 15

Dave drove to Georgetown. Julie the maid answered the door. He pushed his way into the house.

"Where is he?"

"Mr. Hunter's in his study, Mr. Cassidy."

Dave strode down the hallway and Julie chased after him. "Wait, sir, he's on the telephone."

Dave burst through the door just as Hunter hung up. He grabbed the man by the shirtfront and slammed him against the wall.

"You son of a bitch! McDermott's got Trish. If he harms one hair on her head, I'll kill you myself, Hunter."

Dave released him, and Henry adjusted his clothes. "That will be all, Julie."

"Shall I call the police, sir?" the startled maid said.

"No, that won't be necessary. Please close the door on your way out."

She gave Dave an apprehensive glance then departed.

"That was McDermott on the phone," Henry said. "I have two hours to give him the money and diamonds, or he's threatened to kill her."

"Where is he?"

"He said he'd call back in an hour. I can raise the money, but I swear, Dave, I don't have the diamonds."

The telephone interrupted them, and after a short exchange, Henry handed him the phone. "It's Bishop. He wants to talk to you." Dave snatched the phone from him.

"Dave, we've got a tap on Hunter's phone and heard the whole conversation. We're on our way there. Don't let Hunter leave."

Dave had all he could do to keep from strangling Hunter until Bishop and the squad showed up. Bledsoe and Williams were with them. Dave was relieved to see the two guys up and around, but all he could think of was Trish's welfare.

"First thing, Mr. Hunter, you are under arrest," Mike said. "There's a federal law against aiding and abetting terrorists. I want the full story from you, and I won't lie to you, you'll have to serve time. I can't promise amnesty, Mr. Hunter, but the more you cooperate with the Agency, the more likely your sentence will be lighter."

"I'll do whatever I can to help. I don't care what happens to me, Mr. Bishop. My daughter's welfare is my only concern."

"A little late for that, isn't it, Henry?" Dave lashed out. "Just tell us where we can find her."

Mike gave him a disgruntled look. "Dave, back off and let me handle this."

"You can get his confession later. Trish's life is at stake here."

"I'm aware of that, Dave. We can't do anything until McDermott calls back. So cool it. Let's hear what you have to say, Mr. Hunter."

"I admit that Robert Manning and I had dealings with Colin McDermott. Robert's trip to Morocco was to exchange two million dollars for the uncut diamonds. It would appear that the night your men raided bin Muzzar's palace, Robert saw an opportunity to...shall we say, go into business for himself. He told me the money and diamonds had been left at the palace. I believed him until the night Robert was murdered. McDermott came here, roughed me up a bit and said he now wanted not only the money, but the diamonds back as well."

The desperation in his voice left little doubt that Hunter was telling the truth.

"McDermott didn't believe that I wasn't in on double-crossing him," Henry continued. "A couple of days later he called and admitted he had murdered Robert, and my daughter would be next if I didn't come up with the money and diamonds. I told him I'd give him the money, but swore to him I didn't have the diamonds."

Dave had been pacing the floor as Henry spoke. He came to an abrupt stop when Bishop asked, "Was your daughter in on this?"

"No, of course not. She had no idea what was going on. She went to North Africa with Robert because he agreed to give her a divorce if she did. Robert had lied to me and indicated they were going to reconcile, so I encouraged her to go."

"It didn't occur to you to ask her if he was telling the truth, did it, Henry?" Dave lashed out.

"I knew Robert wouldn't hurt her, so I didn't see what harm it would do."

"Wouldn't hurt her! You lousy bastard!" Dave lunged

for him, but Kurt and Don grabbed him and held him back.

The telephone rang and Bishop said, "If that's McDermott, keep him on the line as long as you can so we can get a fix on his location. Let him think you have the diamonds."

Henry nodded and pressed the speaker button on the phone. "Hello."

McDermott's voice came over the speaker. "You got the money?"

"How do I know my daughter's okay?" Henry asked. "I want to talk to her."

"There's not time for that," McDermott said.

"I want to talk to her," Henry declared. "I don't trust you."

McDermott let out a string of vile obscenities, and after a few second's pause, Trish said, "Dad." Dave's heart leaped to his throat.

"Baby, are you okay?"

Dave had to force himself not to snatch the phone out of Henry's hands.

"Everything's going to be okay, baby," Henry said.

"Okay, you satisfied?" McDermott snarled. "Now get in your car and head northwest on the George Washington Parkway. I'll call you in ten minutes. And if you're followed, you won't see your daughter alive again."

"I'll come alone. I swear it. Just don't harm her."

"Ten minutes," McDermott said, and hung up.

Bishop pulled out his phone and dialed the Agency. "Did you get the trace? Good," he said, and hung up after writing down an address.

"The call was transmitted from Fairfax County in the vicinity of—"

"Great Falls, Virginia," Dave exclaimed.

"Yes," Mike said.

"He's doubled back to the same house where he snatched her. We're out of here."

"Good luck," Mike said as the men hurried to their car.

"What should I do?" Henry asked.

"We'll put a wire on you, and then you'll follow McDermott's instructions. If Dave is right, the team will get there and be in place before we arrive."

"Are you coming with me?"

"Of course," Mike said.

As the team approached the house through the surrounding woods they discovered the stashed Liberty.

Dave's problem now was getting to Trish before McDermott knew they were there. It would be easy with the manpower he had simply to rush him, but the cold-hearted SOB would probably kill her before they could take him down. He had to get inside the house before Hunter arrived.

Logically, McDermott would remain on the first floor. Dave gave the squad their orders and then he moved around to the side of the house. He saw an entry—an open window on the third floor.

This was an operation the squad had trained for often, even with full packs strapped to their backs. They formed a pyramid. Bledsoe, Williams and Fraser formed the bottom row. Bolen and Addison stood on their shoulders and formed the second row. Dave climbed up to form the peak and was able to grasp the gutter.

He could only hope it would take his weight so he could pull himself up on the roof. If the gutter broke loose, McDermott would probably hear it.

Luck was with them. With an extra hoist from Kurt and Justin, Dave succeeded in swinging himself onto the sloping lower roof.

He then crawled up to the open window on the upper roof. His gun fell to the ground in the process and there was no time to retrieve it. He would have to go in without a weapon.

Dave gave them an all-clear sign, and the men scattered to their positions.

Once inside, from the sound below he could tell that McDermott was in the living room. That meant Trish would most likely be there, too.

He stole down the stairs undetected and reached the first floor just as a car drove up to the house.

Clutching an AK rifle, McDermott hurried to the window.

It was enough of a distraction to enable Dave to cross the foyer unobserved.

"Your da's here, cutie," McDermott said.

That meant Trish was in the room for certain. He had to get between her and McDermott before the squad moved in.

"McDermott," Henry called out from the porch.

McDermott's gaze swept the yard to make sure Hunter was alone and Dave ducked into the dining room when the terrorist moved to the front door to unlock it.

Dave had a full view now of the living room. Trish was bound and gagged, sitting on the floor in the corner.

She saw him and her eyes widened in surprise. He motioned her to silence and ducked behind a nearby couch.

"Where's my daughter?" Henry declared.

The two men came into the living room. McDermott had the rifle pointed at Henry.

"Whether you believe me or not, McDermott, I did not double-cross you," Henry said. "Manning told me he gave you the money and bin Muzzar had the diamonds."

"I've no time for your lies, Hunter. Just hand over the money," McDermott snarled.

Dave started to inch his way toward Trish. If McDermott turned around, he was sure to see him. His movement had caught Henry's attention though.

"Colin, I don't understand why you're doing this," Henry said. "We had a good arrangement set up. I can understand why you killed Robert, but why bin Muzzar? He was our contact."

"Why do you think? I figured he and Manning were trying to pull a fast one on me. As soon as his little army left to chase after Manning, I showed him the error of his ways."

"So they got what they deserved," Henry said. "That's no reason why you and I can't continue to do business."

Hunter was doing a good job of keeping McDermott's attention. Dave reached Trish.

"I don't think so, Hunter. I have to find a different source for money. This country's a little too hot for me. Your damn CIA, the police and the FBI are all on my tail. So if you don't mind, I'll have my money and the diamonds now."

"How do I know you won't kill me and my daughter then?"

"If I'd wanted to kill her, I could have done the same night I killed Manning. I was hiding in the bushes when she came home that night. I should have. I've wasted a lot of time dealing with you."

"Why did you kill Sharon Iverson? She had nothing to do with this any more than my daughter does."

"I thought maybe Manning passed the diamonds on

to her." He laughed lightly. "I'm thinking you're trying to stall with all these questions. You wouldn't be trying a sting on me, would you, Mr. Hunter?"

"You don't have a chance, Colin. The police have the house surrounded."

"Then say goodbye to your daughter before I kill you. They can bury you together."

He turned his head and pointed the rifle at Trish. Dave threw himself on top of her to try and shield her just as McDermott fired. The shots went wild when Hunter grabbed McDermott's arm and started to wrestle the weapon from him.

The gunshot triggered the squad into action and they broke in, Bolen's shot hit the terrorist in the heart, but not before McDermott had turned the weapon on Henry and fired. Both men fell to the floor.

Mike Bishop had come in with the squad and was bending over McDermott by the time Dave freed Trish.

"McDermott's dead," Mike said.

"Dad!" Trish rushed over to her father. Kurt was kneeling over Henry. He looked up at Dave and shook his head, then got up and walked away while Trish cradled her father's head in her lap.

"Somebody get an ambulance," she cried out.

"There's one on the way, Trish," Bishop said.

"It's too late for that, baby," Henry gasped. "I'm sorry, honey. I almost got you killed."

"It doesn't matter, Dad. Just hold in there. You'll be okay once we get you to the hospital."

Henry tried to smile, but he was slipping away quickly.

"I'm sorry I've fouled up your life, honey." Tears were streaking Trish's cheeks. "Don't let me do it any longer. Do you hear me?"

"Yes, Dad, I hear you."

"There's so much I want to say to you, honey. And so little time to do it. I've been so wrong."

"Please, don't try to talk, Dad. Save your strength. Just lie still until the ambulance arrives."

"It's better going out this way than spending the rest of my life in prison."

His voice had sunk to a mere whisper. Trish had to lean closer to hear him. "You've got a good man there. Hold on to him, baby." He closed his eyes.

"Dad!" Trish cried.

Dave knelt down and felt for a pulse in Henry's neck. "He's gone, Trish," he said gently. He tried to raise her to her feet, but she shrugged off his hands.

"No. Go away. Leave me alone. All of you leave me alone."

Trish mentally closed herself off from everyone in the room and sat rocking back and forth with her father's head in her lap.

They returned to Georgetown and the doctor gave Trish a sedative to put her to sleep. He advised everyone to leave.

Dave refused to go. He sat at her bedside the rest of the day and throughout the night. He could tell by her restless tossing that she was having nightmares. Once there were even tears rolling down her cheeks.

He was suffering his own nightmares watching her struggle. He wanted to climb into the bed and hold her. Despite how he felt toward Henry Hunter, he had never wished the man dead—for Trish's sake, not his own.

In retrospect, Dave realized Henry was not an evil man, only a weak man. And despite the man's other shortcomings, his love for his daughter was indisputable—even if his methods to hold on to her were questionable. But he had died trying to save her—and the way a man dies can often make up for the mistakes of the way he lived.

Trish remained reclusive in the days that followed and throughout the funeral. She not only shunned him, but Deb and other well-wishers as well. She moved about speaking and behaving apparently normally, but those close to her knew differently.

She had lost all interest in the redecoration of her apartment. Knowing Trish's plans for it, Deb took it over and Dave helped her. They supervised the painting and removal of Manning's furniture, and the placement of the new pieces that Trish had purchased. Throughout it all, Trish remained in her father's house.

Dave had watched Trish shrug off the dangers that had threatened her and had often wondered when she would crack under the strain of it. Her father dying in her arms had finally put her over that edge.

And never in the week that followed did she mention her father, nor bring up the subject of where their relationship was going. And he wasn't about to broach the subject. He had every confidence she would eventually pull out of this. She merely needed time to mourn. And Dave gave her that time—and space.

The nagging question in his mind was whether their relationship was over. He'd always figured it would be when the day came that she had to face the reality of her father's past. Now that he feared that day had come, he knew he didn't want to say goodbye again.

Dave actually welcomed the phone call from Mike calling in the team for a mission.

He was stuffing some items into his pack when a

knock sounded on the door. He didn't have time for one of Mrs. Graham's problems tonight.

He opened the door to Trish. "May I come in?"

"Of course." He stepped aside. "I've only got a couple of minutes, Trish. You caught me on the way out."

Trish glanced at the pack he'd put near the door. "You're going on a mission?" Dave nodded. "For how long?"

"I don't know. Three or four days I guess."

"I won't keep you. We have to talk when you get back."

"Yeah, I guess so."

"I've done a lot of thinking this past week. About us. My dad. A lot of things."

"Trish, believe me, I'm sorry about your father. I know how much pain you're feeling." He glanced at his watch. "I wish I had more time. I hate to leave you like this."

"You were going away without saying goodbye?"

"I didn't want to add to your problems. You've got enough on your mind right now."

"I understand." She looked up at him and tried to smile. "Take care of yourself, Dave. We'll have that talk when you get back."

He tenderly cupped her cheeks between his hands. "Goodbye, angel." Then he kissed her. Gently. Tenderly.

Once outside, they walked in silence to her car. He opened the door for her, then said goodbye again. "We'll talk when I get back."

Trish watched him hail a cab. As he climbed in, he turned his head and looked back at her. He grinned and waved.

She remained there, floundering in the force of the anguish of tormented thoughts.

Dave had been right about her father. Had warned her time and time again, but she had always been blind and in denial where he was concerned. She and her father had even quarreled over Dave the last time they were together the day before he died.

Surely he must have known the choices he made could only lead to disaster. What had driven him to commit the dishonest acts? Yet she could not hate him for it.

You've got a good man there. Hold on to him, baby.

Those final words of her father's ran through her mind over and over again.

Could it be too late for Dave and her? Was there too much baggage between them to continue to hold on to hope? Had they let the moment pass?

She turned the key in the ignition and drove home.

Wearily, Dave tossed his door keys on the table and went into the bedroom. He stripped, stepped into the shower and let the hot water pelt his aching bones. He was drained physically and emotionally.

For the past four days he'd been haunted by the memory of Trish's visit before he'd left. He had almost blown the mission in Colombia thinking about it. He knew she had come to tell him they were through. That he was right. That her father would always be a painful memory between them.

Well, dammit, he was wrong. Had never been so wrong in his life. Trish and their love were worth fighting for. He should have stayed and fought for them six years ago. Instead, he had run like a cowardly chicken. Instead of building a life together, he had wasted six years of their lives building bitterness and wallowing in self-pity.

Well, no matter how she felt now, he was going to admit his mistake to her, and beg her to give them another try. Surely they loved each other enough to make it this time.

He'd leave the Agency and get a white-collar job. Trade in combat boots for wingtips. His M4 for a calculator. But somewhere away from D.C. This place held too many painful memories for her.

What if she turned him down? Lord knows he deserved it. He'd done nothing but give her a hard time, despite her attempt to rekindle their romance.

Had he blown it beyond her forgiveness?

Suddenly the shower door opened and Trish stood there with just a towel wrapped around her. Her eyes glowed with the remembered devilishness he knew would always be his downfall. But he'd die with a smile on his face.

Her appearance there told him all he had to know at the moment.

Eventually they would get around to talking it out. They'd assured one another that old hang-ups would never come between them again. But not now. Definitely not now.

"Hi, cowboy. Room for one more?"

Dave grinned, and opened his arms. "What do you think, angel?"

She dropped the towel and stepped into the shower.

Epilogue

Mr. and Mrs. David Cassidy stepped outside the church into a hailstorm of rice. Due to the decorating sensitivity of the matron of honor, Debra Carpenter, the rice, of course, had been dyed to match the pale yellow gown of the bride.

Detectives Wally MacPherson and Joe Brady sat in their car and watched the proceedings with diverse opinions.

"Just like I said, Joe, I like happy endings."

"I knew all the time they were innocent," Joe said.

"Yeah, right, partner," Wally scoffed.

"I was just trying to give you a hard time."

"I knew that," Wally said. "And by the way, Manning's uncle collected his insurance money."

"This sure was one crazy case. Nothing about it was normal. Two murders, CIA, Irish terrorist, twin brothers." Joe shook his head. "I tell you, Wally, I ain't sure I've got it all straight in my head."

"What don't you understand?"

"Okay. Manning and Hunter were funding the IRA in exchange for diamonds. Right?"

"That's right, partner."

"And this IRA guy, Colin McDermott, murdered Manning, Sharon Iverson and Henry Hunter before the CIA took him down."

"He also killed some desert sheik in Morocco," Wally said.

Joe snorted. "And we think the Mafia is bad. So, anyway, this Colin McDermott had a twin brother named James. And James had a wife named Britany. She's the one who tried to kill Patricia Manning. Right?"

"She claimed she was only trying to scare her."

"Yeah, sure she was," Joe said. "So what happened to the twin brother and his wife?"

"Since they didn't do any of the killing, they're being extradited to England. The Brits want them."

"Well ain't you forgetting something, Wally? What about those missing diamonds? Who's got them?"

"The CIA. As soon as they heard about them, they took possession of them."

"How'd they do that? I thought Mrs. Manning—"

"She's Mrs. Cassidy now," Wally corrected.

"Okay, Mrs. Cassidy. Didn't she say Manning had them locked up in his safe?"

"You tell me I'm naive, partner. The CIA has the most sophisticated communication system in the world. It employs experts in cryptography, chemistry, cybernetics and just about every other thing you can think of, as well as special ops guys like Cassidy. You think they ain't got somebody who knows how to crack a safe?"

"So why did they snatch the diamonds?"

"Make sure somebody else couldn't. They're evidence, partner."

"And who do they belong to now?"

"Maybe the CIA will auction them off."

"What will they do with the money?"

"How the hell do I know!"

Wally glanced up at the newly-wed couple on the church steps. His beefy face softened in a smile.

"They sure are a good-looking couple. Warms my heart that everything worked out for them."

"Well, it don't warm mine."

"What's wrong now?"

"Considering the time we put in on this case, the least they could have done was invite us to the wedding."

Wally laughed. "You got no romance in your soul, Joe."

"Ain't you noticed that everybody connected with this case except your two lovebirds ended up dead or in the slammer? What's gonna happen with those two?"

"Like I tried to tell you, Joe. They live happily ever after."

"Yeah, on her father's insurance money," Joe grumbled, and wheeled the Crown Vic into traffic.

* * * * *

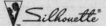
Silhouette®

SPECIAL EDITION™

presents the next three books
in the continuity

MONTANA MAVERICKS

GOLD RUSH GROOMS
Lucky in love—and striking it rich—
beneath the big skies of Montana!

THEIR UNEXPECTED FAMILY
by Judy Duarte
SE #1676, on sale April 2005

CABIN FEVER
by Karen Rose Smith
SE #1682, on sale May 2005

And the exciting conclusion

MILLION-DOLLAR MAKEOVER
by Cheryl St.John
SE #1688, on sale June 2005

**Don't miss these thrilling stories—
only from Silhouette Books.**

Available at your favorite retail outlet.

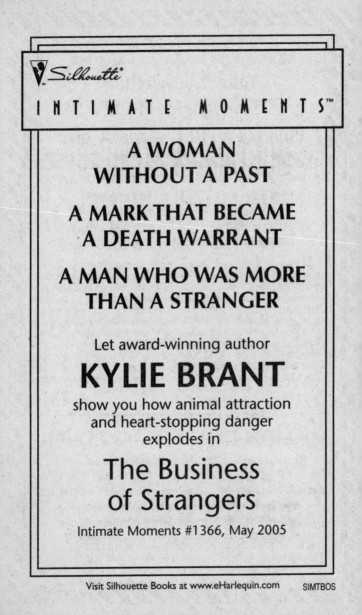

Silhouette®

INTIMATE MOMENTS™

A WOMAN
WITHOUT A PAST

A MARK THAT BECAME
A DEATH WARRANT

A MAN WHO WAS MORE
THAN A STRANGER

Let award-winning author

KYLIE BRANT

show you how animal attraction
and heart-stopping danger
explodes in

The Business
of Strangers

Intimate Moments #1366, May 2005

If you enjoyed what you just read,
then we've got an offer you can't resist!

Take 2 bestselling
love stories FREE!

Plus get a FREE surprise gift!

Coming in May from

Silhouette®

INTIMATE MOMENTS™

and reader favorite

LINDA RANDALL WISDOM

After the Midnight Hour
IM #1367

In homicide detective Jared Stryker's cynical life, the dead stayed dead—until he inherited an old ranch and the ghost who haunted the place. Rachel Bingham had been murdered over a hundred years ago and was doomed to walk the property forever, but when this sexy detective came into her world and awakened the passion within her, she yearned to live again. Jared had never felt tied to a woman, but Rachel's gentle spirit attracted him in ways he never imagined possible...but could they ever find a way to break the curse that bound her?

Don't miss this compelling new book... only from Silhouette Intimate Moments.

Available at your favorite retail outlet.

eHARLEQUIN.com

The Ultimate Destination for Women's Fiction

For FREE online reading, visit
www.eHarlequin.com now and enjoy:

Online Reads
Read **Daily** and **Weekly** chapters from
our Internet-exclusive stories by your
favorite authors.

Interactive Novels
Cast your vote to help decide how these
stories unfold...then stay tuned!

Quick Reads
For shorter romantic reads, try our
collection of Poems, Toasts, & More!

Online Read Library
Miss one of our online reads?
Come here to catch up!

Reading Groups
Discuss, share and rave with other
community members!

For great reading online,
visit www.eHarlequin.com today!

INTONL04R

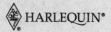
HARLEQUIN®

INTRIGUE

Return to

MCCALLS' MONTANA

this spring
with

B.J. DANIELS

Their land stretched for miles across
the Big Sky state…all of it hard-earned—
none of it negotiable. Could family ties
withstand the weight of lasting legacy?

AMBUSHED!
May

HIGH-CALIBER COWBOY
June

SHOTGUN SURRENDER
July

Available wherever Harlequin Books are sold.